W9-ABN-284

Journey's End

Journey's End

EVELYN BERCKMAN

1977
Doubleday & Company, Inc.
Garden City, New York

Lines from "The Sleeping Beauty" by Edith Sitwell are reprinted from *The Collected Poems of Edith Sitwell* by permission of the publisher, Vanguard Press, Inc. Copyright © 1968 by the Vanguard Press, Inc. Copyright © 1949, 1953, 1954, 1959, 1962, 1963 by Dame Edith Sitwell.

In England, published simultaneously
under the title *Be All and End All*.

Library of Congress Cataloging in Publication Data
Berckman, Evelyn.
Journey's end.
I. Title.
PZ4.B486Jo3 [PS3552.E68] 813'.5'4
ISBN 0-385-12415-5
Library of Congress Catalog Card Number 76-18334

For
Christopher and Deborah Sinclair-Stevenson
dear friends

. . . and in the end
Having my freedom, boast of nothing else
But that I was a journeyman to grief?

Richard II, I, iii, 272

I

The character of the breathing changed toward two o'clock in the morning. At once the priest was on his feet, while one of the female figures in the background melted from the room with the peculiar urgency of the summoner. Of the other two left there one was a uniformed nurse, the other a very old woman, servant of the dying one. Both, as well as the priest, had risen at the warning note of respiration; the nurse taking a sort of quick obligatory step toward the bed, then stopping as quickly in a manner that said, *No use*. The priest on the other hand approached more closely, but his attitude was not of help, only observation. Was this really the moment, the time for the final farewell . . . ? As if in answer the breathing became different again, no longer breathing but another sound, harsh, awful, punctuating the silence with a rhythm strangely regular but running down . . . no longer any doubt, one could not question the death-rattle. At this moment, and just in time, the summoner returned in the wake of two elderly figures in dressing-gowns hastily and irregularly buttoned up. The moment they cleared the doorway they fell on their knees; already the priest was intoning the great exordium of the Church, *Profitiscere anima christiana de hoc mundo* . . . "Go forth, Christian soul, out of this world in the name of God the Father Almighty who created you; in the name of

13

Jesus Christ son of the living God who suffered for you; in
the name of the Holy Spirit . . ." and meanwhile the other
sound went on with inexorable pendulum regularity but slow-
ing still more now, fading, fading . . .

The room was empty, the bed rigorously straightened, the
body so small and withered that it only made a faint ripple
beneath the blankets that concealed it; on the upper part of
the ripple had been laid a crucifix. Everyone, after the long
hard watching—night after night of it—had withdrawn to re-
sume sleep.

Only the priest was awake (actually the priest was a bishop)
being driven the eight miles to the house of a brother cleric,
where he had been given a bed. As the old car bumped over
the rural roads, secondary roads or worse, he was still thinking
of the dead woman but companionably as it were, in the
manner of thinking peculiar to the aged which does not anticipate much of a separation; he himself was well into his eight-
ies, and Mara (he had never liked her real name, Amaranthe,
nor its abbreviation) had been . . . how much older than
himself? A good eight years, ten? His first and predominant
feeling—of content at being able to help her along the last
road—gave way presently to the odd circumstances that had
brought him from Paris in his unsteady old age. The servant's
request, incoherent but urgent: *elle veut vous dire quelquechose, quelquechose* . . . a *something* which seemed to her of
desperate importance, obviously; she would confide nothing
to her two daughters, she wanted her old friend the bishop,
no other priest but him. And obediently he had compelled
himself to the journey, arranged for a lodging in a neighbour-
ing presbytery, endured the motor trip to and fro . . . and
had got there, finally, too late. Much too late to hear the secret, whatever it was; she had not even recognised him for all

the three days that he was there; already she was sliding into the final shadow . . .

He drew an unconscious breath of exasperation and resignation both. His poor old bones had been put to the trouble of the journey for nothing. Still, it could not be helped. The "secret" she had wanted to disclose, perhaps it was no more than the desire to make her last confession to an old friend, and from him receive absolution. Nothing very important in that confession surely, she had always been a woman of harmless but growing eccentricity, disliking her daughters of course but otherwise fairly affable; a tame ending to a family line strongly traced from the tenth century. They had boasted a . . . a field marshal was it, under Louis XIV? or going further back, even an ambassador, he remembered vaguely, perhaps to the Holy Roman Emperor? Well, no matter, no matter, it was all over now . . .

His mind turned—hazily, for he was very tired—toward the matter of the estate. Not a great deal of money left, he would guess. But paintings, antique furnishings? Or had she sold a good bit of it already, out of crazy caprice or out of need? During her long, long decline (for she had begun to be alarmingly strange from her early seventies, as he remembered), she had entered into an immense forgetfulness of everything she possessed, even of who she was at times. One cause of this deterioration might have been lack of money; of all worries, one of the most gnawing. Nor would she have asked assistance from her daughters, not as she felt about them (and no wonder, he admitted). No, she shut off most of the chateau, shut herself off from everyone (himself included), and lived God knows how . . .

Also he had learned very little from his talks with the maid Clémence, in the last few days. Mostly an endless tale, it seemed, of a frail old woman rummaging in the library, keeping up a witless search till the very moment of her stroke, apparently; sad, all of it, sad foolish bygones . . . He began hoping she had left some sort of security to the old servant who had stuck by her. Surely some adequate amount could be realised from a property once so valuable . . . ? He would make enquiries about it, this was an important point and he would not forget . . .

Also he remembered, with a new sharpness (things were coming back to him that he had not thought of for years), that somehow this particular house had largely escaped the pillaging and destruction visited on such places during the Terror; being so near Paris as it was, the chateau had served the upper Revolutionaries—Danton, Robespierre and the rest of that lot—for secret conferences, or as a sort of rest-house or retreat. And for what a crew, betraying and butchering each other in the best Orleanist tradition, for all they were nothing but lower-grade lawyers or tradesmen or diseased scribblers like Marat . . .

In memory of them, the house should have been burned down; it was defiled. Mara had said that, he remembered. But the house was still standing, it had outlasted Mara, he thought with a mirthless chuckle. And even suppose she had sold furniture or paintings out of it, there was still the library; neglected in all probability like the rest of it but perhaps full of valuable books, documents—?

Something pulled him up short, expelling from him a sort of gasp. Yet what for, why, he could not put his hand on it . . . the impression faded beyond reach. Now it was joined by a strange feeling in his head, a curious blanking and floating away, but no pain, not the least vestige of pain . . . he was still fighting, with a weak tenacity, to nail that escaping thought, compel it forward . . . *Library*: it was this word, he was almost sure, that had resurrected some ghost or other: a ghost unidentifiable, having not even an outline . . . yet wait, wait, something was coming back to him, something . . .

Had it been three years ago, four . . . ? At any rate she had begun writing to him after one of her many long silences. Excited letters, incoherent, difficult to read to begin with: lunatic handwriting on soiled paper, pages of disjointedness all testifying to one fact if to no other: she had more or less lost the power of sensible communication. After a perfect hail of such epistles he had taken to protecting himself in the only possible way—by making no reference to her nonsense but chatting pleasantly, soothingly, on inconsequential topics. And mon dieu, her response to these measures! pages of abuse always wilder and wilder . . . In the end he gave up trying to decipher them, tearing them up after glancing at the first few lines. Now it struck him, what had she written about? What had she been trying to tell him? *Library* echoed strongly in his mind once more, it must have been in connection with the library . . .

A new swimming was in his head, a curious emptying in his frame, especially in the major joints; in his shoulders and wrists he felt a coldness, airy yet freezing, and along with it there crowded upon him a tremendous complexity of sights and sounds from the past, yet having nothing to do with one another. The voice of the nun, for instance, showing sightseers through parts of her ancient convent, and he merely another sightseer, a young theological student. Yet he remembered as if it were yesterday her fervent voice telling of Revolutionary profanations, he remembered the horrified murmur of the crowd at some special atrocity, he remembered the nun's shaking hands lifted to heaven and her repetitions of "Les hérétiques, messieurs, mesdames, les hérétiques!" as full of outrage as if *les horreurs* had been yesterday instead of two centuries ago. Now why remember a thing so long gone, it had nothing to do with anything . . . yet naggingly his mind dwelt and dwelt on it, there must be a connecting link somewhere, if only he could find it . . .

Suddenly another change was upon him. In some strange way he was acutely aware, and in another strange way completely detached from his awareness. As his body seemed to fail, to slip away and away, his mind burned all at once with a dazzling clarity. He even recognised the significance of this phenomenon, but the recognition was eclipsed, shoved to one side as memory came back to him, full and clear. He recognised too the connection with the nun, she had spoken of manuscripts, religious works and hand-notated music destroyed by the mob, and all at once like a thunderclap he saw —as if it were before him—one of those crazy letters from half-crazy Mara. She had been rooting in the library apparently and claimed to have found . . . now exactly what? some correspondence of the Léovil field marshal . . . no! the ambassador, ambassador, but not to Austria; perhaps to the Vatican or, as it was called, to Rome . . . ? Unable to remember at the moment, he moved on to the question of what she claimed to find, or at least to be on the track of. Something he had dismissed as more of her wild and idiotic fancies, with growing pity trying to follow the delusions in her scrawl . . .

The answer that burst on him all at once brought with it a vicious thrust of pain in his head. He ignored it, excited and uplifted by incredible vistas. Yes, yes, he remembered now; and if it had been in her mind all these years, it must have some actuality. What had she wanted to tell him? that she had found it, or found some positive clue to its whereabouts . . . ? Whichever it was, and even if it were only a bare possibility, he must notify someone. Tomorrow at the earliest possible moment he would ring the sisters for the name of their lawyer, get hold of the man and warn him of the circumstances, warn him urgently . . . The pain came again, a splitting in his head, a great surge of blinding light and blinding blackness combined. Yet subordinate, all of it, to his moment of triumph, of recollection against odds, the very greatest odds which were time and old age . . .

The car had now reached the presbytery, the young priest who had volunteered to drive him got out and came to open the door.

"Monsieur l'Evêque?" he murmured reverently, then saw that the bishop was huddled in his corner asleep. No wonder, he thought, considering the old man's age, his recent exertions, the ride at this time of night or rather morning . . . a little louder he repeated, "Monsieur l'Evêque?" Peering at the motionless figure, all at once a different accent, a mounting alarm, were in his voice. "Monsieur l'Evêque? Monseigneur? Monseigneur!"

II

The attractive man, not in his first youth, performed his usual assessment as they entered the room. Two bloody old hags (he had known they would be old from the great age of their deceased mother) who were going to be bloody hard to deal with; long experience had made his split-second estimates unusually accurate. Then he was waiting for the one who had corresponded with his employers to disclose herself; probably the one walking quickly and decisively in advance of the other, though perhaps not . . .

"Good morning," this first one addressed him in English with only a slight accent, and the second woman echoed her also in English, but with palpably less fluency. At once the man judged this foremost and taller woman as the correspondent and (perhaps) leading spirit of the two, with whom most of the business would be done.

"I am the Comtesse Marsigny-Villars," she continued. (Yes, he had been right.) "And this is my sister, Mme Cotteret."

He bowed again and stood waiting as they seated themselves, the Comtesse saying in the same moment, "Pray sit down, monsieur." As he bowed a third time and resumed his chair she continued, "You are M. Dominic Godfrey? You have, I suppose, some proof of your identity? I have the Palgrave letter of introduction, but one hears of such terrible things nowadays." Her tone was semi-apologetic. "Such misrepresentation—"

"Indeed, Comtesse." He was on his feet once more, withdrawing a wallet. "You are perfectly right to assure yourself of whom I am." He opened the wallet and turned a number of cellophaned pages slowly before her.

"Thank you." Her scrutiny had been sharp and thorough. "One understands that in a case like this, where objects of great value are perhaps concerned, one must take nothing for granted."

"Indeed, Comtesse," he repeated. "Nothing must be left to chance."

"Alors," she nodded as he resumed his seat, then paused for the evident purpose of collecting her thoughts and the not-so-evident purpose of entertaining some thoughts of her sister. *Look at her, the fool,* she snarled in parenthesis. *A young man, and at once she begins smirking and ogling. At her age, three years younger than I, and I am seventy-two.*

"Monsieur Godfrey." The mere sound of her voice, very clear for all its harshness, very composed and direct, again gave him essential information. The two of them were probably co-heirs, but this old battle-axe was the leading spirit. The other one's simpering and bridling had not escaped him (very few things escaped him), but this one was the businesswoman of the two. No trace of a smile out of *her,* no fear; not a vestige of anything but a grim hewing to the line.

"This is a curious affair," she was saying. Now evidently decided on her course, she had become fluent. "Our mother has recently died here in the family chateau, at the age of ninety-three. For the last twenty-five years she has wanted nothing to do with us, with my sister and myself; she has shut herself up and lived God knows how. Money should not have been the trouble, but we knew little of that, of anything in fact . . ."

She seemed to wrest herself from an old and troubled chapter. "She had her own maid and sometimes a cook, I believe, in this enormous place. I may tell you that . . ." she hesitated, then plunged on. ". . . we made enquiries years ago in regard to her sanity, but . . ." Over her second hesitation she made a gesture. "Right or wrong, the decision went against us."

And since then she hasn't been so friendly? he thought with an inward smile. *Odd, dear Comtesse, very odd.*

"She made us look like fools in the lawsuit," the younger sister put in, speaking French. "*Comme des niais*, she made us look."

The glance that the Comtesse threw at her sister, a half-glance only, was enough to startle him with its quality—not only of family ill-will, normal, but of actual enmity; withheld perhaps but there, flourishing and even deadly.

"I tell you of this situation and of our mother's behaviour," she had resumed smoothly, "to explain the condition in which you will find everything." She drew breath. "We have been through the chateau quickly, Mme Cotteret and myself, and—!" She flung up her hands, a despairing gesture. "What she has sold or given away, what has been stolen or spoiled I cannot tell you, no one can tell you. But I wished you to understand that the state of things is not my—is not our fault."

The visitor's discreet voice spoke only after a pause.

"Thank you, Comtesse," he murmured gently. "Such neglect and so forth is by no means unknown to us in our work. However—" he paused delicately "—these conditions will necessarily impede investigation, slow it up, which will of course increase Palgrave's fees in proportion. I thought, Comtesse, it was only fair to mention this."

Another pause fell, curiously awkward; he only had time to notice that once more the younger woman was simpering complacently, when the elder replied, "We know." She seemed affected by a sort of strangulation. "Mme Cotteret is making herself responsible for all fees."

The smile on Mme Cotteret's face deepened, and once more the stranger had a lightning perception: by her silence the younger sister had forced the other to admit not only to this arrangement, but to the fact of the elder's poverty. A feeling of embarrassment made him add quickly, "I would suppose at a guess that all your furnishings and art objects, at the best, would only date from 1800 or thereabouts? The chateau would have been looted, of course, during the Revolution?"

The pause, this time, seemed rather a surprised one; at the end of it the Comtesse said vaguely, "I am not quite sure, I mean about the looting. Marie, would you know . . . ?"

"Maman would have known." Obviously Mme Cotteret understood the English conversation, and as obviously understood the purpose of her sister's enquiry. "Maman was always reading. My sister and I—" she gave Dominic a coquettish glance and the Comtesse a poisonous one "—we were never much for the books." In characteristic weak-minded fashion she veered to another subject. "We have had an *ambassador* in our family."

"Indeed, madame?" he said politely. "In what period?"

"Oh, long ago, very long ago."

"This is a matter of your *expertise*, not ours," the Comtesse addressed him stonily. "You yourself will find out these . . . periods and so forth."

"Of course," he agreed submissively, then heard behind him the sound of an opening door, of someone entering and— after a permissive gesture of the Comtesse—taking a chair.

"So this is understood." She continued speaking Engish while making the gesture. "You will commence your investigations at once then, and lose as little time as possible—?" She paused only for his nod, then pressed on, "Now, as to the library. I understood, monsieur, that Palgrave's were to send with you an expert in books and such things?"

"They were, Comtesse, and I apologise for this delayed appearance. Actually this expert is my wife, who is just recovering from an attack of flu. Not serious," he added hastily at her expression. "She will be here in two or three days at the latest. I apologise again for this circumstance," he repeated dulcetly, "but it could not be helped."

"I see," said the Comtesse after a moment, thin-lipped. "Well, I have arranged that you will stop here in the house during your recherche; this is not a neighbourhood for hotels. The old servant, our mother's former maid, will do you meals of some sort."

"*If* Clémence stays on," Mme Cotteret added slyly.

"I have already ascertained that she will stay on for a while," said the Comtesse coldly, and at once it was Mme Cotteret's turn to become thin-lipped.

"There are plenty of chambers *à deux*," the elder resumed. "I have already given orders—"

"Comtesse, I beg pardon." Dominic had not interposed with any degree of haste, yet to one person in the room there was an undercurrent about it, intangible. "I would beg for separate chambers, if it is no inconvenience. My wife much prefers being on her own, when she has just been ill."

"Oh." The Comtesse picked this up at once. "Do you mean that she is often ill? habitually?"

"By no means, Comtesse, by no means." The haste absent from his request was now fully in evidence. "Simply, when she is not quite herself she likes to be alone, but illness of any kind is rare with her."

"That is fortunate. Well, two bedrooms are no difficulty in this place—" she broke off suddenly and began speaking in French. "M. Reval, there is no need for your presence after all, just at the moment. When the library expert arrives, one will notify you."

Again there was no least word from the presence behind Dominic; nothing but the almost inaudible sound of someone rising, retreating, and the door closing softly. On the heels of this small episode, however, a wry look had appeared on the elder sister's face.

"Our mother . . ." she had returned to English, on a perceptible note of constraint. "One of her habits was to pick up various strange creatures, men and women both, and allowing them to stop here for a while. Even long ago, when she would let us visit her, my sister and I have found these persons living here—not a thing to give one tranquillity, *dieu le sait*—!"

She stopped, evidently under pressure of disturbing thoughts.

"This young man whom I have just sent away," she continued abruptly. "He is the latest of the series. He tells me that maman employed him as a *librarian*." The contempt in her voice was qualified, as if not quite sure of its ground. "For all I know he is really a librarian, I am no judge. So I—so *we*," she corrected herself hastily, "have permitted him to stay on, until the arrival of your wife. If she does not find him of any use, she has only to tell us."

Dominic, with the talk straying from his own specialties, nodded unhearingly; questions of his own had begun rising in him.

"And in this case," the Comtesse was pursuing, "we will get rid of him at once."

"Comme il est beau," the witless voice of Mme Cotteret put in, on another smirk. "Vraiment un beau garçon."

"Well then, M. Godfrey, if this is all for the present . . ." The Comtesse, not looking at her sister, managed to convey a freezing contempt. "You have come prepared to begin at once?"

"I have come prepared to make a preliminary survey, and to report to my employers," he said cautiously. "If they judge it worthwhile, they will entrust the whole affair—the preliminary cataloguing, the packing, the transit of the cases to England—to my discretion. On the other hand, if my report is disappointing, they will terminate the arrangement at once."

"One would hope so," Mme Cotteret said unexpectedly. "Especially when one reflects that I am paying the bills *pour ces préliminaires*."

"The account would be presented promptly, madame." As he switched to French he noted with a shade of malice that the reference to expense had silenced the Comtesse, at least for the moment. "Especially since Palgrave's, as usual, are overwhelmed with work."

"But you agree with me, with my opinion?" The Comtesse, along with her urgency, had recovered assurance. "If the things are auctioned in London, there is much more chance of high prices—?"

"Undoubtedly, if they are first-rate," he replied, again with caution. "Auctions in London or New York are likely to command the very highest prices."

"As I thought." She flicked a glance of undeveloped triumph at her sister. "Well then, I shall tell Clémence two bedrooms. She is old, but not too old to be useful—Oh, by the way." There had been something false, or at least awkward, in her manner of breaking off. "I had almost forgotten to tell you. You will please not use any of the fireplaces even when it is chilly, the chimneys have not been cleaned for years. We have almost had a fire, you will have noticed the smell?"

"Hardly at all, Comtesse, I took it for a smoking chimney, something of that sort." He had noted how she avoided her sister's eyes on making her request, and the sister's slight smile and bridling that indicated where the responsibility for the incident lay.

"So you will remember?" the Comtesse was saying commandingly. "If you please, monsieur?"

"Bien, what did I tell you?" The Comtesse had reverted to French. "An auction in London is the only possible thing."

"You have told me ten times." Mme Cotteret's asperity changed all at once to a whimpering. "But the jewelry, Monique, the jewelry—!"

"Mon dieu!" her sister cut her off. "Who will know, who can possibly know? Will you stop bleating about the jewelry?"

"But Maître Dalbert—"

"He? Why should he know? He is only a lawyer after all; he is not a diviner or a magician. He has probably not set eyes on maman for years, and beside—" her voice swelled positively "—he is ill. He was even ill at the time that she died. A mercy for us, and let it go at that!"

"Yes, but he will be better one day. He will be coming here." With unusual resolution Mme Cotteret supported her opinion. "Maybe at any time now."

"Well, and if he does? Do not be ridiculous, Marie." To the Comtesse's habitual contempt was added impatient finality. "A client who is a recluse at best and half-crazy at worst—does such a person keep lists? inventories?"

"Who knows?" The other's voice combined retreat with tenacity. "One cannot be sure—"

"Marie, for heaven's sake cease! Let Maître Dalbert come, I am ready for him.—And now that we have the Englishman here, and the wife about to come . . ." She had gone from temperish to calculating. "—we had better look a little to our own comfort, have our rooms *really* cleaned—" She broke off.

"That is, if you intend staying here during the experts' recherche—?"

"If you stay," her sister answered comprehensively, "*I* stay."

"As you like," shrugged the other.

"After all—" Mme Cotteret, with a resumption of spite, flourished her one useful weapon "—who is paying for these experts?"

"You are." The embarrassment of the Comtesse was over and done with. "For a sum which is nothing to you, *nothing*, we have the chance of a world-famous auctioneer and of getting ten times, twenty times, what we might get otherwise."

Mme Cotteret was silent a moment, then with habitual flightiness went off on another tangent. "He is handsome, the *anglais*." She started to giggle, then asked midway, "But why does he not love his wife?"

"Let us see about our rooms." The elder sister was elaborately weary and disdainful. "And about getting in food."

Dominic, after the ancient and untalkative maid had indicated the two big rooms side by side, carried his two cases and briefcase up a superb flight of stairs, and dumped them thankfully. Then oddly enough, and without inspecting his quarters further, he hurried to the communicating door and looked. To his profound gratitude the key was in it; he locked the door and withdrew it, putting it in his pocket till he could find a good hiding place. Only after this did he look the room over without interest, glad of somewhere to sleep on the premises instead of driving to and from a hotel. A portentous double bed, oversized chests of drawers and two wardrobes, an offensively ornate dressing-table, all this exuberance of 1855 framed by brocaded wall paper in uneven pink. Then he sighed and stood, for a moment, in deliberate suspension of thought. Into this hiatus strayed a question, unimportant, which had not occurred to him previously.

Odd, I shouldn't have thought it would be allowed—those two harridans staying here while Val and I are working. Still, I'm not up in French laws of inheritance to that extent.

He sighed again, took from his briefcase a fat notebook, and set out for a first survey of this completely unknown domain.

III

The young woman whose husband was in love with someone else, and whose identity she could not even guess, shifted miserably in her bed, then shifted again to her former position. What did one do against a horror like that, what did one do . . . She moaned unconsciously and lay still; not thinking precisely, only letting a hundred half-thoughts, half-recollections, go drifting before her. What should she do, it always came to that . . . still, men did get over these fancies and return to their wives, were even *glad* to return. And the job in France was waiting and here she lay an inert lump with no will, no desire, to move. Yet if such a job had come her way when things were normal, how interested she would have been, how excited even . . . but something else had snagged her attention: some word she had just used . . .

After a moment she had pinned it down: *normal*, that was it. At the sound of it an onrush of thoughts and feelings, never before acknowledged, came flooding out of concealment. Had her marriage—two years old—had her marriage ever been right? Now that she forced herself to look things in the face, no, it had not been right, not ever . . . with unaccustomed resolution, shrinking only a little, she set herself to face and define the wrongness. And now that she had brought herself to the point of probing, while ignoring the sickness at her heart, all at once it was clear, destroyingly clear. Dominic had married her while in love with someone else, that was the whole thing. He had lost someone with whom his inmost fibre had been engaged, and had married to exorcise the memory of loss; restore as much as he could the wound, the open lesion . . .

"It didn't work," she said aloud, was startled at the sound of her own voice, then went on trying to guess at the nature of this loss. Not by death, she would think; loss by death, being irreparable, seldom held the survivor in *unbreakable* chains. Well then, the girl had loved and married someone else; it was from this he was unable to recover. *Two years*, she reflected with despair, *during our two years he's got worse, not better* . . . A stab of clairvoyance suddenly invaded and tore her apart. *He's met her again*, she thought. *And this time she's not inaccessible, her own marriage has gone wrong or something. What a fool I was not to see it before, what a hopeless fool* . . . *he's my all, my all*, she prayed silently, ground to nothing between millstones of absolute knowledge and useless hatred, *Oh God, Oh my God.* Jealousy ripped her apart like a claw. *Who*, she panted to herself, *who is she?* But conjecture was no use, he was always meeting women in the course of his profession, beautiful or gifted or wealthy women . . . She lay motionless, seeing him: the arrestingly handsome face with its high forehead, the black hair breaking over it in beautiful strong lines, the level grey eyes above prominent cheekbones, the firm mouth; the tallness, the body that moved with such grace and control . . .

"Oh no!" she gasped aloud, "*No!*" Blind panic had forced it out of her, the thought of loss. *He may get over it, he may,* she continued thinking, *I'll wait, I'll wait, I'll be patient* . . . From mere violence of misery she sat up violently and threw back the covers. First groping for her slippers she got out of bed and struggled into her bathrobe while staggering a little, partly from her depth of despair and partly from genuine weakness.

His exploration of the house, the preliminary summing-up, had taken the better part of two days. Now, descending from the attics at the west end of the chateau, which he had reached last, he moved in a sort of stupor, a sleep-walking unbelief. To find what he had found up there, stowed away out of use and out of memory . . . He administered a mental kick and forced himself awake. A phone, a call to London . . . the house phone was the last he thought of using; the village, puny as it was, must have a public *appareil* somewhere. By now, going downstairs at a quicker rate, he almost ran full tilt into someone coming up—a man in this rookery of women, to his vague surprise; he had certainly not seen him before . . . Then he remembered the librarian slightingly discussed by the Comtesse, at the same moment that both of them were sidestepping with agility. "Pardon, monsieur," the unknown had murmured.

"My fault, my fault," Dominic replied absently and unseeingly. He dodged around the other and pelted down even more rapidly, savouring what he had to communicate to his employers; it would knock them back, there was a tingling and crepitation all through him at the thought of his news. This would be an enormous operation, bidders from New York and all over Europe, and himself the discoverer, the leader of the enterprise . . . Then beside the enormous advantage to Palgrave's there was the favourable effect on his own position in the firm. A directorship, say? and at no distant remove? And how this would strengthen his own situation, in the trouble that he saw coming nearer every day, always nearer . . .

"Jeremy? Dominic here."

"Ah yes." Whether an instant chill fell on the voice or not, the caller had no time to decide; the importance of the call brushed aside such minor considerations. "How're you getting on?" Jeremy had continued.

"Not too badly. Actually, could I speak to your uncle? I did ask for him."

"He's a bit tied up at the moment, I'm afraid. If you'll tell me what's on your mind, I'll—"

"No," Dominic interrupted with force and no apology, an unusual combination for him. "I must speak to Mr Palgrave himself. If he's busy now, I'll ring later. Put me through to his secretary, could you, and I'll ask when he'll be free?"

"But you could tell me—"

"If you *don't* mind," the other interrupted again. "Just get me his secretary, could you?"

There was a silence, brief but loaded, then a series of clicks and another silence—long enough to let Dominic reflect, with a sardonic and reminiscent smile, on Jeremy's coldness, and the near-certainty that this coldness came from an old jealousy. In love with Val had he been, all that time ago? except that someone had cut in ahead of him. If only it were so; if only she would fall back on that dreary fidelity, what a heavenly release . . . "My God," was forced out of him, aloud, by his longing. "My God if only she would, if only . . ."

"Dominic?" A voice heavier than Jeremy's came through, the voice of an elderly man, and at once he responded, "Yes, sir. Good day."

"And how're you getting on with your *shat-to?*" The pronunciation was part irony, part bad French. "Anything in it?"

"Anything?" Dominic echoed, and took a deep breath. "A fortune, sir, I should say. Several fortunes."

"Eh?"

"You see, sir, it's a rather remarkable set-up." He wet his lips for an extended effort, after the startled monosyllable. "I don't suppose you'd run into it anywhere—except Portugal maybe or some of the old aristocratic Spanish houses. This place was a sort of resort for the top Revolutionary men, Robespierre and his crowd, so the mob didn't get hold of it like so many others." He drew breath again. "Then the original owners got it back apparently, and it's been in their hands ever since."

"Mmm! you don't say."

"So I've been through it quickly," the other resumed. "Just to get an impression. It's not a huge chateau, just medium, but there's enough to turn you dizzy. Did you know, sir, that the last owner, this Mme de Léovil who's died recently—did you know she's been crackers for the last twenty years or more?"

"Yes, the daughter hinted at something of the sort—the daughter who wrote."

"Well, so putting aside the neglect and ruinous condition of the ground floor and first floor, there's . . ." He took another deep breath, shaky. ". . . there's one end of the attics . . ."

"Yes? yes?" His voice had galvanized the listener, apparently; it sounded like a double bark. "Yes?"

"They're crammed . . . simply crammed . . ."

"With what? what?"

"Pieces from 1630 onward, I should say." He had control of his voice again. "And a scattering of good stuff in disused rooms, servants' bedrooms and so forth—I've been through all of it pretty thoroughly." He paused for an instant. "Apparently they just shoved the stuff up there as new-fashioned furniture came in. There're masses of horrors from the Exhibition of 1855, and so on."

"But this attic stuff, you say—?"

"Originals from Louis Quatorze and Louis Quinze mostly." Again the thought of it brought back a slight constriction in his breathing. "No large pieces, no cabinets. But chairs, tables, étagères, mirrors, first-rate so far as I've gone."

"Paintings?" the other demanded. "What about paintings?"

"Family portraits, mostly. By Largillière and so forth, not absolutely top people but good; they all need cleaning—I haven't really gone into the paintings yet. But—" he made a sound, a sort of laugh. "—but furniture in stacks. And what we'll find when we come to unstack it, God only knows."

"And the library?" The elder Palgrave's voice had sharpened suddenly. "There's a library?"

"There is one, in a frightful mess apparently—I only glanced in there for furniture or paintings. Very bad luck," he complained, "that Val's been held up."

"I've just been having a bit of a chat with her." The old man's voice, all in an instant, became affectionate. "She's up, for the first time today. Talks about setting off for France tomorrow, but of course that's nonsense."

"Still, so long as she's got that far—"

"You'll see," the old man interrupted. "You'll see when you ring her."

And who told you I'd ring her, he answered silently, then woke again to his employer's voice.

"Now," it was saying. "How d'you think we ought to do it?"

"Well, sir—" All at once he was calm, assured, decisive; this implied recognition of him—as an expert—was a wonderful feeling. "—as far as the canvases are concerned, perhaps you'd consider having them auctioned in Paris." The suggestion so carefully worded, he thought, could carry no offence. "They might find a better market there than in England, since they're portraits of a family not famous or anything. But the furniture—" This time it was joy and excitement that stopped him for an instant. "—the furniture's a different story. Of course the upholstery's done for with dirt, moth, mere passage of time—" he gestured unconsciously. "And in a good many pieces where glue was used the glue's perished, or other pieces are shaky for other reasons. It's an extreme risk," he concluded, "to try shipping it over, in its present condition."

"All right." Mr Palgrave was decisive. "How should we handle it?"

"Well, this is a case for the best people you've got—"

"Norbert? Phil?"

"Norbert if you will, please, but I think Alex instead of Phil—a repairman who's also a first-rate crate-maker and packer. Norbert for the more important repairs and reinforcements, enough to let the things travel—that's the most important."

"Right, I'll send Nor and Alex. When you tell me—?"

"Splendid, sir, thank you. In one or two more days I'll have time to really see what's there, set aside the more important pieces to begin working on, and so forth."

"Right. Well, goodbye, I'll—" the elder Palgrave stopped suddenly. "You didn't examine the library? Not at all—?"

"Sorry, sir, I didn't." The old boy and his furious passion for books, he thought; exactly like Val. "I was just looking for stuff in my line. It's in shocking disorder, that much I can tell you—someone's been through it like a rocket, but who or when I don't know. It's one great big room and a small room, more of a closet actually." All at once the thought of the librarian struck him; what sort of person would let his charge go to ruin so irresponsibly, disgracefully . . . He put the thought aside and offered the old boy something to feed on. "Still, one never knows—if there's anything good, Val'll turn it up."

"She will." Mr Palgrave's voice held a profound conviction. "That girl."

41

He drove back to the chateau with fierce, barely controlled impatience. The attic, the attic: he could not wait to get up there again, to begin his real assessment of this cave of riches. He had reached the outer gates before he knew it, tall gates now sagging badly and permanently open. The neglected road with its bumps and dips he hardly noticed, his mind already in the house with its secret, unknown treasure . . .

All at once he braked, the abrupt motion so in advance of what had caused it that only a full moment after was he aware of this cause. Through a gap in the overgrown trees and bushes that lined the avenue, under the brilliant sunlight he had caught a glimpse of pale colour that after a moment resolved itself into a living body. Or half a body rather, from the head to the waist, sitting at such an angle that the legs were invisible. All the same this body was naked, he had the strongest feeling that it was altogether naked. The head, brilliantly blond, was bowed on the arms folded upon the knees; every other thing about it—the suppleness of the back, the clean shoulder-line, the quality of the pose—suggested youth, even extreme youth.

With his mouth suddenly gone dry, his heart beating suddenly hard, he sat rooted and staring. This must be the one he had almost fallen over on the dim staircase, less than an hour ago; presumably the same person who had been called to his initial interview with the old women, then dismissed without his having set eyes on him; the librarian so slightingly referred to by the Comtesse, and by what he could see of him now a boy, the merest boy . . .

He remained completely still another few moments; the apparition, fairly distant and also perfectly still, seemed unaware of him. Again he started driving, this time slowly, partly absorbed and partly astonished by his devouring emotion. Unless it came, of course, from the long months when he had done without, when he had not dared indulge himself except

for the most fleeting adventures, stealthy and cruelly unsatis-
fying . . . ?

Within a few yards of the chateau he braked again suddenly, turned the car, and drove back fast to the village tele-
phone. His sudden need to ring his wife was the result not of
thought, not of affection, but of instinct not to be put in
words. Suppose she descended on him soon, too soon; suppose that such a descent might prove inconvenient in case
. . . in case that . . .

"Val?"

"Nick!" Along with her reasonless surge of joy came the
memory that he hated this abbreviation. "Dominic," she continued on a considerably chastened note, "how lovely to hear
from you."

"How are you, Val?"

"Oh, I'm all right."

"No." Impatiently he dismissed small talk. "How near are
you to getting in motion? coming out here?"

"Well . . ." Her voice faltered a little. "I was going to start
tomorrow or the day after, just full of ambition you know,
but . . ." She turned apologetic. "I'm not so good as I
thought, after all."

"The doctor's forbidden—?"

"Oh Lord, the doctor couldn't stop me if I felt up to it.
No, it's my own wretched miserable . . ."

"You're not up to it." He made it a statement, not a question. "Not yet."

"No, I'm afraid not."

"Well." His voice became less curt, with immense and unconscious relief. "All I wanted to tell you—in case you're held
up a week or even more—don't worry. There's so much to do
here, it can't make any difference."

"You mean—" Interest had brought her voice to life again. "It's something good? big . . . ?"

"You might say that." Now that he knew what he wanted to know, his only anxiety was to cut this short. "I think it's pretty good."

"But tell me—the library, you've seen it? Does it seem to amount to anything?" All at once, her professional passion coming to life, she was pelting him with questions. "Would there be a muniment room? Were you able to notice if—"

"No," he broke in flatly, all at once on edge. "There's a library, it's all I can tell you—it's your affair." He paused, suddenly realising both his tone and the quality of the silence. "But you're better?" he essayed awkwardly. "You're really better?"

"Yes," she said in a dull voice. "Much better, thank you."

"Well, keep it up." He was frantic to get away. "See you then, when you can make it. 'Bye!"

"Goodbye," she said, on a note barely audible. It made no difference; he had rung off.

Reckless with a sense of escape, he drove fast. His hunger for exploration of the house had given way to a different hunger, which he fought not to acknowledge. All the same, once past the gates he went very slowly, and when he came to the same cleft in the foliage, stopped once again. No one there, this time; no one . . . Starting the car once more, he was transfixed by a question. What was it, on first sight of this . . . boy? man? *boy* sounded more accurate, let it be boy. So what was it he had felt? Not only the fierce desire to see his face; there had been that too, and yet . . . after a moment he had it. The naked upper back bent far forward, the bowed shoulders; not bowed to get the sun on his back, no, but from grief, unhappiness . . . He sighed heavily and unconsciously. A bond was already between him and the faceless object, a kinship of trouble. *His face,* he thought again, *I wish I could have seen his face,* then felt—strangely, simultaneously—that the face was beautiful, but if it were not it would make no difference, no difference at all. Or again, perhaps this moment of strange excitement was all he was going to get out of it; no more than that . . .

Chilled and slowed by the thought he locked the car then turned toward a side door, the only one in use apparently; the stately front ones topping the stone staircase seemed permanently closed. Once inside, he ran full tilt into the Comtesse. She had a disorganised look, he noted at once; the look of one who wants to plunge into activity, give orders right and left, yet forced to be inactive, to wait upon forces outside her control; he knew something of that feeling himself.

"Bonjour, monsieur," she greeted him abruptly. "Have you examined, well, commenced your examination? Do you have any idea of the—the value, the possibilities—?"

"I think so, Comtesse." His answer was prompt; actually he was obliged to tell her of developments—while shading his account lest he himself had been a little too sanguine. "I have spoken to Mr Palgrave our principal, and from what I have seen so far—" he hesitated slightly "—I have discussed with him the advisability of sending two cabinet makers, one of whom is also a packer, to see whether the objects can be prepared for shipment or not." On this lie, designed to keep her in check, he saw the instant alarm in her face.

"Two helpers?" she shrilled. "But monsieur, an expense of this kind, *épouvantable,* I do not know if my sister would consider this, this—additional—"

"Be tranquil, madame," he interrupted boldly. "I can assure you that such expense will be covered, more than covered, when the objects are sold."

In a flash her expression had changed from uncertainty to

hungry hope. "You mean the things are valuable?" she asked, palpitating. "That you—you anticipate the big prices?"

"For some of the things, I should say quite good." Again he was lying or half-lying, automatically protecting himself from clients' feverish expectations. The prices would be enormous, undoubtedly, but give these old harridans an inkling of how enormous, and he would have on his hands a couple of mad dogs. *Mad bitches*, he amended silently, while continuing, "With things so old there is always the question of decay, which I am not competent to estimate. Not so competent," hastily he amended another lie, "as a first-rate cabinet maker would be."

She was silent; accurately he divined the furious greed, furious curiosity, furious impatience in that silence. Serenely he waited for the next manifestation, almost sure of what it would be.

"These objects are of Louis XVI?" she demanded.

"Earlier," he had to acknowledge. "Considerably earlier."

"Ahhh." A sound long-drawn, sated; she was smiling, the faintest inward smile. "Aux greniers? in the attics?"

"Yes, Comtesse."

"Could I see them?" she demanded. "Just to look?"

"If you do not mind, madame, it is better not. The stuff is piled up dangerously or lying about, the dirt and dust are incredible. It would be . . . *safer*," he repeated firmly, "not to."

She nodded after a moment, with extreme reluctance.

"Shall I also tell Mme Cotteret?" he pursued with relief; she had not tried to pin him to values. "Of Palgrave sending over—"

"I will tell her," she interrupted. "She is not here at the moment." Her mind had evidently veered to something else; she asked an unexpected question. "You have said that these objects are heavy?"

46

"Have I, Comtesse?" he smiled, wondering what next. "Actually, some of them are very heavy."

"Well, but you might need assistance in moving things of that sort?" She was incisive again. "I have told you there is a young man here, fairly idle I am sure. Let him help you." Without waiting for his assent or otherwise she had put herself in motion, marching ahead of him; he followed dumbly, in a sort of trance. "At least let him earn his bread a little, why should he not . . ." Talking more to herself than to him she had reached the lofty double doors of the library, seized a knob and opened energetically. "Monsieur Reval?" she called at once, loudly. "Monsieur Reval? Où diable est-il?"

On the last sentiment, in which she had not troubled to lower her voice, a figure appeared from behind them on the left, and stood there silently.

"Ah, vous voilà! Bien, here is Monsieur . . ."

"Godfrey," Dominic helped her out, seeing that she had already mislaid his name.

"—ah yes, M. Godfrey who needs someone upstairs, where he may encounter things heavy to be moved. You will please help him." The imperious phrasing and tone of voice made Dominic quail. "You will not be occupied here till the library expert has arrived, no?"

"No, Comtesse," the presence replied submissively.

"Good. Then you—" she had turned to Dominic "—will tell M. Reval what you require." On this note of explicitness, she swept from the room.

"I beg you." At once Dominic addressed the unmoving figure in its own language. His heart had begun beating up into his throat hard enough to shake his words a little. "There is no need—" he continued, then stopped. "Do you speak English?" When the figure shook its head he continued in French, "Do not trouble yourself about these directions, I implore you. There is no need to help me, I am not moving

47

heavy things especially, only looking at them." Those eyes, black beneath the blond mane, the chiseled lips, the face absolutely unlined like marble, the purest marble . . .

All the same he must be cautious, the statue might be mad on girls, there was nothing to show one way or the other . . . Yet an overwhelming desire not to lose sight of possible felicity pushed him into continuing, "Still, if you are not too much occupied, and if these things interest you, I would be glad of your assistance when you can spare the time."

"Thank you, monsieur, you are very kind."

The mere sound of this churned his excitement to a higher pitch. That voice not so much soft as . . . as *distant*, that was it, remote and with the slightest reediness . . . *Pan's pipes*, he told himself, his thoughts in chaos, *the pipes of Pan* . . .

"I would be very glad to help you," the alluring accents went on. "I know nothing of these matters which you are investigating, but I am to your disposition." He paused an instant, then added, "Entirely."

"Well, thank you, actually I could use assistance at times." The final word had set his head spinning additionally; did he mean anything by that *entirely*? Also he needed no assistance like this, unskilled . . . "We might begin now, if this is convenient for you—?" As the other bowed and came forward submissively he shouted in silent and sudden rage, *Don't be humble for Christ's sake, I can't bear it!* "Books are your entire concern, I suppose?" he continued his tentative exploration, somehow at a loss. "Your passion?"

The boy, as they passed out of the dim library into brighter light, gave him a glance as he said, "One might say yes, my passion," then muttered something inaudible.

"I regret," Dominic said politely. "I did not hear you—?"

"It is nothing, monsieur."

The unheard phrase—it sounded like *not books, a book*—was overlaid, again, by its mere vocal quality; that combination of softness and alienness, like a poetry almost forgotten . . .

> *. . . old as tongues of nightingales,*
> *That in the wide leaves tell a thousand*
> *Grecian tales . . .*

Edith Sitwell, yes; as it came back to him the other was continuing, "Nothing at all."

As they began ascending the stairs, Dominic—somehow without the courage to glance outright at the strange companion—all the same was registering other impressions. Young, young, the most exquisitely lissome body, the pallor that defied exact definition, as skin-colouring sometimes did; the palest ivory, tremendously vital, contrasting with the blond hair and blond eyebrows, the black eyes . . . then he was belatedly aware of his look of poverty, jacket and trousers shabby, the shirt limp, the shoes cracked and scuffed. But the skin and hair clean, brilliantly clean . . .

By rights he should always be naked, he thought. *Naked down to the tops of the legs, the fur on his thighs his only covering, with hooves instead of feet.* Also his glance, his atmosphere, not entirely human . . . ? By now the catalogue had evoked in him an excitement so overwhelming that he could hardly breathe, and yet—

He might be girl-mad, he reminded himself with an unpleasant tension in his head, an equally unpleasant constriction in his breathing. *Careful, careful, be careful.*

IV

"But Comtesse," said Maître Dalbert. His voice was of the mildest; years of experience had taught him all there was to know of the behaviour of legatees. Well, not *all*, he could still be a little surprised by human behaviour under the stress of money-greed. What he had accomplished, however, was a technique that was proof against the most feverish avarice, the wildest impatience, or mere bad manners; a gentleness and endurance immovable against any exhibition that clients chose to make of themselves. Nor were these two old women the worst he had ever encountered, not by a long shot . . .

"You see," he continued addressing them both in his most persuasive voice, a little muffled by his recent severe cold, "if you and Mme Cotteret had *always* lived here, or lived here at intervals over a term of years, certainly it would be your right to remain here during the settlement of the estate. But since this is not the case, regretfully I must beg you to remove from the house as soon as possible. Very regretfully, mesdames, but—" He shrugged. "There it is."

The polite ultimatum was followed by a pause; after it Mme Cotteret said, "And to think I must remain here in some wretched local inn, when I have a comfortable apartment in Paris."

"You need not remain, Marie," said the Comtesse. "I shall be here to keep my finger on events."

"Many thanks, Thérèse." A cryptic quality developed in Mme Cotteret's tone. "But I also, I shall remain here myself."

Another pause, minimal but awkward, followed this pronouncement.

"Very good then, maître," the Comtesse agreed sourly. "There may be a slight delay while we enquire about rooms in this unpromising neighbourhood, but otherwise we shall go as soon as possible." Her decisive voice, her action of beginning to rise, signified the end of the interview. Maître Dalbert, far from accepting this gesture and rising too, seemed on the contrary to adhere more firmly to his seat.

"A thousand pardons, Comtesse," he said in a voice of extremest apology. "But there is first another question or two, if you do not mind . . . ?" As she paused in surprise, then sank down again, he was aware of the change in her expression. A wariness, sudden . . . ?

"I have here," he continued, opening his briefcase, "inventories of this house in general, and very detailed ones of jewelry, paintings, sculptures and other objects of value. It is true that some of these inventories are old, but on the other hand those of jewelry and objets d'art are recent. Made a year ago," he added, "at the express direction of Mme de Léovil."

Having detonated this bomb he paused an instant, then continued speaking against a dead silence.

"Now if any person whatever, even the heirs, had abstracted any of these objects—any at all," he emphasised delicately, "before the final settlement of the estate, I must point out that they would expose themselves to severe official penalties." He paused again. "So I must ask you, mesdames—" *if you've helped yourselves, greedyguts that you are*, came irresistibly to his mind as he continued with irreproachable courtesy, "—if either of you may have removed any such things, of course for reasons of safety or caution or—"

"You are quite right, maître." The Comtesse had recovered her poise along with her fluency. "We discovered—"

Mme Cotteret made a sudden sharp movement; the other proceeded, elaborately oblivious, "—a jewel box, a clumsy affair lined with velvet, you know it I suppose?" As he nodded she went on graciously, "We took charge of it simply to ensure its safety, you understand, and we are very pleased to be relieved of the responsibility. But to have an object of such value simply lying in one of her closets, to which any thief would go first thing—"

"You are quite right, Comtesse," he agreed cordially. "But you may now hand me this box and absolve your mind of the burden. All of it is there, I trust?" His eyes went from one to the other. "*All?*"

"If one or two bits have somehow strayed," said the Comtesse grandly, "we shall look about and put them back." She threw a deadly but guarded glance at her sister who had made a sound, an undeveloped snort as it were. Simultaneously Maître Dalbert had said, "Many thanks, madame." *In a hurry, such a hurry to divide the loot,* he thought tiredly, and pursued aloud, "And the objects such as paintings, drawings, chinoiserie, they are also intact?"

"Oh surely, surely," said the Comtesse with such unconcern that at once his mind charged her with abstracting—say —one or two of the *smaller* canvases. Not that anything all that valuable was in this collection, so far as he knew, but both as a point of honour and a matter of personal dislike he would see that they kept their harpies' claws off it till the last of the legalities, the very last, were completed—

"*We* should be executors." The voice of Mme Cotteret, more harsh than silly for once, broke into his reflections. "Not a bank, a parcel of clerks whom one does not know."

"The Provençal et Midi," he returned mildly, "beside being

your mother's bank for many years, is of the highest reputation."

Mme Cotteret sniffed but was reduced to silence. Not so her sister, who pushed in rather too quickly with, "Alors donc, maître, all is understood perfectly. We shall withdraw from the house and find lodging elsewhere, however inconvenient this is. But the law, the law!" She gave a tinkling laugh; a falser sound the lawyer had never heard in either of his two lives, personal or professional. "It must be obeyed, no?"

"Hélas, as you say, madame." If she thought he was through with them, she had another guess coming. "And there is no other object you have prudently safeguarded, Comtesse? Nothing at all?"

The faintest check, imperceptible to most people (Maître Dalbert was not most people), touched her before she replied graciously, "Only two small paintings, maître, and a bust, a tiny little affair—"

Already he was turning over pages of an inventory as she sang on mellifluously, "—almost a sort of toy, not likely to be worth anything—"

"Yes," he interrupted in the dryest voice; he had not interrupted before. "The head of a young girl, late seventeenth century and signed by Houdon. I know little about these things," he digressed, "but I should say that this miniature size would make it extremely valuable. I have seen other Houdons, but always life-size or nearly."

"I see." The Comtesse got up with the rapidity of escape. "Then Mme Cotteret and I will let you know our whereabouts as soon as we have found some *logement*—"

"And the two small canvases, Comtesse." He had no intention of letting her off the hook too soon, feeling an unworthy pleasure at her every wriggle and evasion. "By what painters?"

"Heavens, I do not know." She had become defiant. "I

thought them a convenient size to hang, that is all. Mon dieu, these formalities! My sister did not wish them and they are mine, after all."

"But now that you have heard the will you know that the bust and two paintings are willed to the Musée Marsigny. It is possible that these are the paintings." No animal so voracious as a widow, he thought, while replying with an unction so deadly that it got home even to her; she bridled a little. "Actually these objets d'art were inventoried a year ago, at the request," he continued even more dulcetly, "of Mme de Léovil herself. She had a good many sane and sensible moments, you know." He inclined himself with special courtesy and picked up his briefcase. "Mme la Comtesse, Mme Cotteret, I have the honour to wish you a very good day."

"Well?" began Mme Cotteret, almost before the door had closed on him. "What did I tell you—"

"*Shhh!*"

"You!" Pleasurably the bullied ignored the bullier, for once. "You with your *nobody will know, we will divide these things ourselves!* So nobody knows!" She crowed with squalid enjoyment. "Nobody—"

"Be quiet! It is done and over—"

"And the paintings!" The glee of the upper hand was not to be relinquished in a hurry. "When I said better not touch them, *who* said they were small, *who* said no one would miss—"

"This was before the will was read to us! Let us now consider where we are going—"

"Comtesse de Sait-Tout!" shouted Mme Cotteret. "She can be wrong like everyone else, she can—"

"Shut up!" The ferocity of the elder (as always) finally drove the younger into silence. "Shut up, do you hear? And now come!"

"Where?" gabbled the other, relapsing into feebleness. "Come where . . . ?"

"We must talk to this man, must we not, the *anglais?* tell him we are going? You would have us run away with no word? Allons!" The Comtesse's ascendancy, contemptuous, was already re-established. "We must find him."

"I see," said Dominic, grave and respectful. "I see, mesdames."

"We shall be nearby, however," said the Comtesse on a note of warning. "We shall find something near. But I and my sister have decided between ourselves that it is better, perhaps, if we remove from the chateau."

"This may be wise, Comtesse." *If she isn't lying,* he thought, *I'll eat my hat.* The arrival of the good-looking car he had not seen, only its presence when he came downstairs for a smoke. But he would bet anything that the lawyer or lawyers had slung the two old girls out of the house. "Since my employers are sending these two men to help me—" he continued, and was interrupted by a shriek from Mme Cotteret.

"*What?*" she demanded. "What do you say?"

"These things must be prepared for transport, madame—"

"Two men!" she screamed like a peacock. "Who pays? And you have not asked my permission, not consulted me even—"

"Madame!" he got in ahead of the Comtesse. "The objects are fragile, many of them, they must be examined with the greatest care, temporarily reinforced if necessary. I cannot possibly hire stray labourers from hereabout, only the most expert workmen should touch them." She had become ominously silent; understanding that silence he said in a hurry, "Such incidental expenses will not be billed till after the auction, in any case."

The half-stupidity of her face had changed to a look of deepest cunning; the same cunning loaded her voice as she asked softly, "Then these things . . . that you have found up there . . . they are valuable?"

"Objects of these epochs are always valuable, madame," he said. "As the Comtesse has already recounted to you."

"No one has recounted me *anything*." She sounded stifled, while giving her sister a curious look. "*You* tell me."

Oh Christ, you old bitch, so the other old bitch held out on you? Aloud he answered, "I believe we should get a good attendance at the sale, madame, and I believe it will go on for three days at least, even four."

"Yes." She spoke softly, her eyes distant and rapt. "Of course I have read of such in the papers. You will have buyers from all over the world, millionaires—?"

"I believe so, quite possibly."

"Alors, Marie," her sister broke in. "We have detained M. Godfrey long enough from his work." Her extra-smooth tone indicated her knowledge that she would have to make, and make promptly, some sort of explanation. "So we had better —Oh!" She broke off suddenly and turned to him again. "I had almost forgotten. This young man who was going to help you, you remember? He cannot now be of use to you, since your assistants are coming, so he had better leave at once. I will tell him, therefore." She paused, reflecting. "And that is all, I believe—"

"Comtesse," he put in fast, as she was turning away. His voice was casual, against his urgency of actual fear. "Pardon, but when the library expert arrives I believe he will be of service, quite necessary service—"

"Ah yes, your wife," she interrupted. "I had forgotten. When is she coming?"

"In the next couple of days, certainly." How curious the after-echo, to himself, of *your wife*: in so short a separation the words already alien, having nothing to do with him . . .

"She has recovered, then?" the Comtesse was saying.

"Oh yes, madame. It is certain," he murmured, "that she would be greatly helped by the presence of the resident librarian."

"If you tell me so, bien," she shrugged, and he began to breathe again. "He need not go immediately." Her face had changed to the same slumbrous look of greed as her sister's, her voice to the same purr and rasp of greed; for the first time he saw the family resemblance between them.

"Imagine," she was saying. "I had almost forgotten the books. Very valuable, they would be—?"

"That, I would not know."

"You have no idea? None at all?"

"No, Comtesse." He was deferential. "Books are not my province, malheureusement."

"I shall go to London, to the sale," Mme Cotteret was screaming on her way to the door. After her silence during most of the colloquy, it burst out of her like steam from a kettle. "The Connaught or Claridge's, I shall stay there. For me only, do not think I will pay such rates for you. If you had not tried to be secret about the *valeurs* I might have had you stay with me, but as it is no, *no*, this is all your cleverness has brought you—"

For all the other's efforts at suppression, her jackdaw's voice continued coming back to him till mere distance silenced it.

Over the third cup of coffee in the village estaminet he continued sitting still, with the total stillness of thought continuing or thought reviewed. The house would be empty of the harridans presently; but what would be the effect of this emptiness on his present bondage? The infatuation (after so long without one) that lay on him like stone; the pain that lanced him on any first sight of its object after an absence however short; the breathlessness and stammering that he had to control in the presence of this object . . . To say nothing of his lost appetite that was making him noticeably thinner, and his smoking which had shot up from moderate to excessive.

Then—above all—was his consuming uncertainty in regard to the central point, his inability to tell whether the boy (very highly sexed, he felt certain) were after all woman-bound. Make the mistake of an advance to one of that kind, and it was simply a question of what ruinous trouble he had brought on himself. Police and newspapers at worst, blackmail at best . . . his head swam as he considered the possible result on his business career. Especially considering the nature of his employer, a full-blooded widower who up to a couple of years ago was having it off with his secretary and possibly others at the same time . . .

He walked back to the chateau; for the torments that beset him, he needed to walk. A face was before him as he strode along mindlessly, a face smooth, changeless . . . peaceful? no, not peaceful . . . "Inhuman," he said aloud, trying to find some handhold against the flood that was drowning him. If only he had *some* indication; one glimpse of the presence in company with a girl would be enough. And that would be the end, the end, however it destroyed him he must get over it as well as he could. After all he had his work here, there were still tons of it, thank God; his mind would be occupied, at least during the day. But the nights, the nights . . .

On a groan almost soundless, with the vacant eyes and sagging look of the leaden heart he had reached the chateau. This adventure, infatuation, whatever it was—already he had given it up, he told himself. But it resisted death, it wanted not to die, this emotion of such force as he had never known before, no never. Or again, did this ardour merely come from the two years when he had fought to suppress his natural instincts? And with hardly one downfall, hardly one . . . ?

A blankness extinguished him; the saving blankness of impasse. Feeling nothing, knowing nothing, he was going up steps without end. Steps of marble, of highly polished wood, last of all of rough board gone splintery, smelling powerfully of dust and leading up to semi-darkness. This first room of the attic was empty, the men must be at lunch. Silence of death, total, like the death within himself . . . A faint chink recalled him; mindlessly he followed the sound past the next two partitions where he had shoved a valueless table and a couple of chairs. Here the boy sat, working languidly at a bag of collected fragments, gilded wood, bits of tinted marble, brass mountings come loose, sorting them into separate piles; these bits and pieces would be invaluable to the cabinet makers.

"Hullo, Maurice-George," said Dominic politely. He had advanced no farther with the faun than to call him by his Christian name, and indeed had compelled himself to a manner, rigorously formal, which he felt as his only safeguard under the circumstances. The faun, responding, moved his lips in his peculiar smile which was not a smile at all, and again dropped his eyes to his work. Dominic took the other chair, trying to think of what next; there was something about this mysterious creature which discouraged conversation, at any rate perfunctory conversation.

"The two old women intend to go." He felt forced to say something. "Did you know?"

"They have gone," Maurice-George murmured, without looking up. Carefully he straightened a string of crystals from some bygone chandelier and laid them with similar fragments.

"Already?" said Dominic, startled. "Did you see them go?"

"Heard," said the faun. "One could not miss."

"You mean—" Dominic ventured a smile "—a noisy departure?"

"Screaming," said the boy. "Like pigs being killed."

Dominic smiled more broadly; the other, never looking up, was so totally devoid of any answering gleam that the smile lost its quality of forced amusement, became meaningless, vanished. Meanwhile, something happened; a narrow lance of sun, all at once striking through a bull's-eye window, lit the boy's head and shoulders like a spotlight purposely focussed. Struck dumb all at once, mindless, Dominic stared and stared at a perfection manifest and magnified, as it were, under this fierce scrutiny. The skin vitally pale and flawless, stretched so tight over his features that even in this blinding glare not a line was visible; over his eyes, cast down and showing the long lashes, two fine black strokes level rather than arched; the lips at once sensual and refined, firmly closed and with a deep indentation beneath them, above a sculptural chin; the expression aloof, secret, and something else . . . cruel? was that it, cruel . . . ?

Have mercy, the older man prayed silently, *have mercy*. His heart was tearing him to pieces, he was on the verge of some desperate extreme like going on his knees in beggary, mindless beggary . . .

Without warning the faun raised his eyes from his work. Their glances locked, remained fixed for time long or time short, measureless to one of them, not both. Also measureless to the same one, forever with no quality of *when*, was the motion of the young hand, the left hand lying on the table, that now turned where it lay till its palm was uppermost, but slowly, slowly. Then with no least further motion, with his gaze still impaled on the other's, the boy sat waiting.

V

"But you know absolutely nothing about the comfort, nothing about what facilities are available there—"

"The comfort doesn't worry me," she tried to stem the flow.

"—a house where the owner's been a sort of lunatic for years, it must be shockingly run down—"

"All I need is a bed of some kind, one can always pick up food somewhere or other—"

"—and you still far from well." They were interrupting each other constantly. "Anything but well—"

"Uncle Frederick," she drove in. "Did Dominic say it was uncomfortable?"

Brought up short, Mr Palgrave seemed to cast about, finally admitting, "Well, actually he's said nothing about it one way or the other. Still," he recovered rapidly, "comfort and convenience mean little to a man in good health. But you, my dear, a girl just getting over an illness—"

"I'm fed up with my illness," she said ruthlessly. "As soon as I've work to do—" *As soon as I've set eyes on Dominic,* clamoured her inner voice sick with longing, *as soon as I'm near him. He may be different after all this while without seeing him, everything may be different* . . . "Something to take my mind off myself," she was continuing. "That's what I need." Ruthless again, she bore down his protests. "I'll be all right, dear Uncle, I'll be perfectly all right."

Between the two men lying side by side there were unexpected resemblances, for all the violent difference of their inner and outer nakedness. They were alike in their exhaustion, alike in the blackness of *after*, and alike in their secrecy; each was keeping back something from the other. Yet with the older man this withholding was accompanied by such dread that it had weakened his potency, of which he was proud; while the boy's hidden absorption, nudging him with wild anticipation and wilder excitement, had made him oblivious to this weakness, over which he would be normally loud and mocking. They continued to lie as they were, no sign at all of their inner tumult, while the silence deepened, deepened . . .

"Well." Dominic broke it finally; he received not a syllable, glance or movement by way or answer. "Well." No answer. He raised himself on an elbow, rallied his companion with a smile, and again said, "Well?"

"I hate this dirty hole," said Maurice-George distinctly, flicking a glance at his shabby room.

"Yes, you've said it before."

"Why," demanded the young man, "can we not use your room?"

"I've said why not." He was brief. "I've told you the reason." That this *reason* had been perfectly false, would have to come out sooner or later. That much he knew; the problem was when to come out with the truth, *when* . . . . The faint cold shiver that traversed him invisibly underlined the other truth that he had not yet admitted to himself: that he was afraid of this cruel capricious little brute, genuinely afraid . . .

"Bah, your room is much better," murmured Maurice-

George, yet absently; again he was oscillating on the swing of his excitement, growing more and more tense, breathless . . . "The books." It was forced out of him, finally; at least he must skate around its outer edges, or go mad. "When will you do the books, the library?"

Dominic, who had lain down, raised himself again; something in the other's accent, some . . . tension? suppression? . . . had snagged his ear and his curiosity. Yet the word *books* brought him close, dangerously close, to his own secret; better tread carefully for a bit . . .

"I don't do the library," he answered. "Books are a different *expertise* from mine, completely different."

"Ah," said Maurice-George, and let his torment drive him a step further. "They will send someone from England, then? an expert for books?"

"Certainly," replied Dominic, and took the lead for an instant; something in the boy's manner, some powerful undercurrent, was distracting him even from his own worry. "Is it a good collection, Maury? Would there be correspondences?" Beside the curiosity that was pushing him on, there was now an automatic professional interest. "Or anything beginning with the fifteenth century?"

"I do not know," replied Maury with utmost composure.

"You don't know!" This brought Dominic up sitting. "But you've been in the library quite a while, haven't you, long enough to—" He broke off again as realisation dawned. "Tell me, are you a librarian at all?"

"Certainly not." He was completely indifferent. "The old cow that is dead, I never told her I was one. She took me in so I could help her with the books, that is all."

"Oh." He thought a moment of the frightful and unconcealed disorder of the library. "What was she trying to do, arrange the books a little?"

"I do not know, she was crazy. Who knows what a crazy woman does?"

"It's that way, was it?" As the boy ignored him, seeming half-asleep, he lay down again, his momentary interest dying as his caution revived stronger and stronger. *The books* would inevitably bring his secret out into the open, he was more than willing to put off the moment as long as possible. Then suddenly he was worried: Val would realise the boy's uselessness in five minutes, she would mention it to the hags of course and they would get rid of the poor young thing without loss of time . . . *Have to do something about that straightaway,* he thought grimly, then woke again to the voice.

"The Comtesse and the other one," it was saying. "They will have money from selling these things? much money?"

"A fair lot," Dominic admitted cautiously, and waited for what next.

"Two old *chiots*, already smelling of the grave," the boy pursued. "And still with their dirty claws stretched out, still talking of what they can get."

"And how do you know," the other enquired, "what they talk about?"

"I listen." He was frankness and simplicity personified. "I listen to them."

"How?"

"In this rotting old place there are a thousand and one holes." Maury was peaceful. "I have heard them talking together fifty times."

"Oh." Along with his amusement was a sort of uneasiness, which he consciously refrained from examining. "I see."

"Women," the faun was murmuring. "Women."

The deadly vitriol of the word, this time, imposed a sort of stop; after it Dominic asked, again with caution, "You don't like women?"

"The old ones I would kill off at the age of fifty at most," said the boy tranquilly. "The younger ones I do not like, but they have their uses perhaps."

The third sex, reflected Dominic. His heart lurched again with sickening cowardice. *Not a pervert, no, but simply of another sex.* He had also seen lesbians so utterly alien to women that the same phrase held good. *Man with his narrow classifications excludes them, but Nature doesn't.* Then he returned to what was coming nearer and nearer, the crisis with what depths of disaster in it only God knew . . .

"Tell me," Maury was saying. His voice and manner, slumbrous, had woken up suddenly. "This expert of the books who comes from London, what sort of person is he?"

The following pause, very slight, was nevertheless crammed to bursting—with Dominic's increased panic combined with attempts to remember. He had mentioned "my wife" during that first interview with the sisters, that much he knew for a certainty. The question was, had the boy been in the room during this mention, or come in after it, or what? The more frantically he tried to nail it, the more it eluded him. Then again, remembering that they had spoken English and that more and more French spoke it nowadays, he was impaled on the next question. Suddenly and without previous intention he asked, in English, "You want an opinion on the expert, do you?" and was met by a look of such complete blankness that he continued, "Tu ne parles pas anglais?"

"Some words." He obliged with samples. "God dam. Fock," and instantly reverted to his question. "What is this to do with him, the man of the books?"

Anglais de salon, Dominic thought dryly, then summoned all his forces to meet the danger head on; no help for it. "The expert of the books is not a man, but a woman. In fact—" ignoring the other's nauseated grimace he drove on steadily, "—in fact, she is my wife."

The instant of dead silence was followed by what he had anticipated. The boy stared at him blankly, then with sudden violence tried to rise and plunge off the bed. Dominic, no less ready than anticipatory, gripped him hard above the right elbow, then managed to get hold of the left one. For a few moments they fought savagely, the boy spitting single words under his breath and Dominic determinedly silent, saving himself. Only when the wild threshing seemed to lose strength a little did he say, "Listen a moment—"

"Non! non! cochon, salaud—"

"—only a moment," he continued with a good imitation of calm. "Listen."

"Get out, get off my bed—"

"Maury, listen, Listen, listen . . ."

The convulsive plunges had abated, stopped—perhaps only for a moment, he reminded himself; the faun lay pinned but glaring, ready to leap up again—as soon as the hold on him relaxed, Dominic knew, but he had no intention of relaxing it.

"We are separated," he began, knowing he would have to lie a little—only at first, he assured himself, just at first. Already those three words seemed to have done him a service; the other's hatred was no longer *pure* hatred, it was combined with . . . a listening? a half-listening . . . ?

"Separated," he repeated the panacea. "But she is employed by the same firm who employ me, and I cannot help it —that they are sending her on this job. I cannot help it," he repeated. The ten thousand thousand shadings of the human face, he could not help thinking; the boy's look of enmity becoming less implacable but still there, ready to leap back at a wrong word, one single wrong word . . .

"I haven't slept with her for six months," he blurted, falling back on truth. "For over six months I swear, Maury, I swear it."

He waited, too lumbered by subservience to remember that he was still pinning the other down; when a temperish movement reminded him he took his hands away and again waited, his eyes riveted to the other, painfully . . .

"She is good, the woman? very good?"

Nonplussed at this unexpectedness, he took a moment to sift its meaning from several possible meanings.

"Her occupation, you mean, her work? Oh yes, very good indeed." The unconquerable veracity that dominated him in his profession made him add, "She would not be used by Palgrave's if she were not one of the best, the very best." Then he was taken aback, also completely puzzled, by the vanishing of the rage so wild and mindless only a moment ago; what wrapped the boy now, or seemed to wrap him, was a brooding about something else; nothing for it but to hold his breath and wait . . . "Her father was a scholar and a collector of books," he added uneasily. "Quite well known in his day."

The eyes returned and fastened on him; recognisably Maury's eyes, yet with something in them that still held him at a distance.

"Why," asked the boy hostilely, "did you marry this woman? or any woman?"

"Well." Since this was a query he had anticipated moments ago, he was more or less prepared. "Well, first of all, she is on excellent terms with the owner of our business, the old Palgrave."

"His *amie*, you mean? his mistress?"

"My God no, he was a great friend of her father, she has known him since childhood—a family friend."

"I do not understand," said Maury coldly, "why you married her for such a reason."

"I'm ambitious, my love, I'm frightfully ambitious. This firm of Palgrave is an old family affair, a thing hard to break into. She's one of the directors, so it seemed a way in—a step in the right direction." He ventured a bleak smile, and went on hastily when there was no return, "Then also the woman has a good lot of money, and money always helps."

"She is rich, you mean?"

"Not rich but comfortable, very well off. When her father died she gave part of his collections to various universities and museums, but the rest she sold off to great advantage. And in addition to what he left her, she has money from her mother. Well off," he summed up. "She is very nicely off."

"Yet all the same, she works?"

"Lord yes, she adores it—has a passion for it."

"How old is she?" In the question was a flat antagonism ready, but held in reserve. "A hag? older than you, much?"

"Oh no, younger." He saw at once that this had created displeasure, but no help for it. "A couple of years younger."

"And she loves you?" came softly, balefully. "She is in love with you?"

"Yes." A bad question, but no dodging it. "She is, and—" Surprising himself, it came out violently. "—I couldn't stand it any longer!" he snarled, and flung himself down. "I couldn't—!"

"Leave her."

"Well . . ."

"Leave her," Maury repeated in a soft unmoved voice. "Why not?"

"There are reasons."

"What reasons?"

"For God's sake." He began to be temperish under this bland pressure. "The thing can't be broken off just like that— there are various issues, complications."

"What complications?"

"Well! For one thing, I've told you how she is on good terms with the *patron*, as close almost as a daughter. If I give

74

her the push, he will give me the push." He glared. "Now do you understand?"

"And so?" Maury shrugged. "You will get another job."

"Ha! much you know about it. Palgrave and two others in London, they are the chief concerns in all the world—even in New York is not their equal. Anyone thrown out of such establishments must go lower, not higher, there is no help for it." He threw another defiant look at his inquisitor. "And I am very well liked there, *installé*, I am entrusted with bigger and bigger affairs, in three or four years I may be a director. One does not throw all that away, I assure you!" Then at once he was uneasy, partly with a sense of having betrayed his own position too clearly, and partly dreading a show of bad temper to match his own. What would he do in that case? climb down—?

"You said—" The boy was nothing worse than meditative, to his relief. "—you said a moment ago, *for one thing*." He moved his dark slanting eyes sideways. "The other things, the other complications, what are they?"

"Well . . ."

"Do not constantly say *well*."

"All right, all right. Well, another—Oh, *pardon*. Another reason is, when we return to London and you come with me—" he stopped suddenly. "You are, aren't you? coming with me?" The faun's eyelids descended enigmatically; afraid to press the question he hurried on, "We have a nice house, she and I." He was aware all at once he could not call her *my wife* any more. "Or rather it is her house, inherited from her father. If I continue to live there I can afford a small flat for you, where we can be together a great deal. If I leave her at once, we will both be living in one or two rooms. For you, I wish something better. Also if I remain with her I would have more money to spend on you." Again he glanced hopefully at the other's face and thought, *Beautiful. Impassive like a statue, beautiful . . .*

The sculptured lips opened and asked, "And you really do not fock her?"

"I have told you I do not," Dominic said heatedly. "Not for months, now."

"And she stands for this?"

"She is patient." Disgust wried his mouth for a moment. "Dieu, how patient! Then lately she fell sick, thank God, and the question did not arise."

"Ah," said the faun consideringly. "But she will not endure this forever, to be celibate."

"That's just it." His unwillingness to reply was matched by real astonishment. This young, young creature, how he could force him to reveal not only his most secret plans but also his most secret weaknesses! From whom else would he have stood for it? From no one, in all his life before. "When it comes to that point, sometime in the future, it will be she who wants the divorce, *she*. Compris, alors?"

"No."

"The *patron*, little fool, the *patron*. How can he blame me, if *she* throws me out? And I know her, she will never tell him why, she is too modest. She will ask for a hearing in chambers, a hearing not public, if I know anything about her. So my job will be safe, that is the great point. And by then I shall be paid more, it advances year by year, and we will be happy and comfortable."

"But how soon does all this arrange itself? How long will this woman remain *pas fockée*, without pushing the loud screams?"

"Quite a while, I told you she was patient." He sat up, the annoyance in his face giving way to something else. "And now, *mon gars*, I must talk to you seriously."

"Dominic." Ignoring him totally, the boy was off on another tangent. "Est-ce que tu me preteras ton auto?"

"Lend you my auto?" He was as completely side-tracked as surprised. "What for?"

"Oh, pour faire des petites excursions. Also I love to drive, I love it."

"Well, nothing doing." He was immovable. "Sorry, but I can't lend it."

"Why not?" It sounded dangerous. "Why not?"

"First because I need it all the time, it's part of my business. And also in the next two or three days, I shall be meeting *her*. Now stop that silly business—" again he had arrested the faun's rapid retreat from him with force equally rapid "—and listen. Listen, I tell you!" His hard voice matched his grip. "I'll have to meet her because I don't think she can drive her own car, not yet. And when she gets here—" his hold on the other became more masterful "—you are going to be nice to her."

"I shall spit on her!"

"No you won't, you will be polite and pleasant. Idiot, do you want to behave in such a way that she'll know about us at once?" He shook him a little. "Do you?"

The inimical face staring up at him again suspended—as it were—its hostility, and this suspension offered an opening wedge.

"So you see." Dominic drove into it. "You needn't embrace her, you've only to be agreeable, offer to help her and so forth."

"Perhaps it is better," murmured the faun sweetly, "if you and I do not meet at all while your *wife* is here."

"Nonsense, we'll meet here in your room as usual. They've put her—" the faintest involuntary grimace touched his face "—next door to me, or have I told you?"

77

"No, you have not told me." Maury's smile became even sweeter. "She will visit you at night, *hein?*"

"No, she will not. I . . . I'll be able to deal with that."

"The auto." He had become deadly. "It is hers, *non?*"

"It is mine, not hers." No need to say it had been a birthday present, no need to say from whom. But the resurrection of the topic drove him to add, "I will give you money to rent a car once in a while." Along with the instant uneasy feeling that this capitulation was a mistake in tactics, he thought of something else. "And we cannot eat together when she comes."

"No?" A return of deadliness. "Elle est de l'aristocratie, non?"

"Don't be stupid, did you eat with me when I first came? You'll go back to eating in the kitchen, that's all. How shall I tell her that I hardly know you, if we've been feeding together? And behave yourself while she's here. Will you? will you?"

Uneasily he looked to see the effect of these orders, and then—his need returning overwhelmingly—ventured to reach out his hand, not realising his timid and imploring look.

Again each man, on separating, knew that he kept secrets from the other. This knowledge in Dominic's case was accompanied by a hangover of uneasiness, part of which was the question: had he talked too much about his wife? But this was a lesser thing compared to the other, the major secrecy . . . for with all his apparent unreserve in speaking of his marriage and the reasons for it, he had still not given the real reason: which was his hope, nearly frantic at one time, that by attempting such relationship with a woman he could conquer his natural inclination toward men, strongly in evidence from his twelfth year . . .

The growing failure of this attempt and the mess in which

it had landed him was, of course, a desperately troubling consideration. Yet and strangely, at the moment, his only thought was, *Suppose I had confided that part of it to Maury, suppose I had been that much of a fool* . . . The trouble was the effect the boy had on him, a longing to pour out his inmost soul, to reveal himself fully and keep nothing back, nothing; it must be the effect of his long loneliness, the loneliness of marriage. In imagination he could see himself telling the whole thing to the faun, and he could see—even more vividly—the faun's reception of it: the mockery, contempt, perhaps rejection . . .

The thought of this last set off in his head a violent shock, dizziness, and something else which he recognised. And beside recognising he named it, without pity for himself; it was terror of losing the boy, abject terror.

As soon as Dominic had left him Maury rose from his bed, light and agile—not worn-out like the old one, he thought with the faintest malicious grin—and made for his mirror, the old bureau mirror with its grey shine like lead and its various patches of blackness. Toward this, deadly serious, he bent with the fixity of someone expecting a momentous revelation, and only straightened after a long minute; he always performed this curious mirror-rite after the act of love. When reassured that pleasure had left no lines either at the corners of his eyes or mouth he relaxed a little and—still gazing with cataleptic intensity at the image—allowed his thoughts to wander backward a little, pleasurably . . .

First to the experiment that had captured this latest admirer: learning by careful observation that Dominic usually took his car out around mid-day he had posed himself, stripped naked, where he could be seen through a break in the shrubbery, this break being carefully widened beforehand. Here he had sat day after day, weather permitting, till the sound of the stopped car—stopped for a long minute before moving on again—told him he had been seen; a similar stopping on the way back, which he had observed from concealment, indicated the success of the trap. The quarry's masculine appearance might be a true indication of what he was, one never knew; the faun had had his suspicions but it was best to make sure . . .

With the remnant of a smile fading (he smiled infrequently and almost never for reasons that amused other people) he abandoned the mirror and returned to bed. Stretching luxuriously he began thinking of Cecil—not with regret or anything like it, but only in regard to what he had gained from the young *anglais* with whom he had lived in Paris. A spotty up-and-down existence, but that part of it was all right; his angry grudge at the moment came from the fact that, during the association, he had not managed to learn English. Well, why should he, Cecil spoke Parisian French and he himself hated the English . . .

All the same he had lied to Dominic; he had picked up a *little* more English than he admitted. Bits and scraps, but enough to get the drift of some conversations provided the voices were naturally clear and did not speak too low or too fast or otherwise unfairly obstruct him. His current calculations, at the moment, were fixed on Dominic's means. Not rich, he had only his pay, yet there might be some private means, some expectations . . . ? Also his eagerness to take his beloved to England, it might be sensible to go along with this? for his own purposes, of course . . . ? So wait, he concluded; eavesdrop on conversations between him and this nasty *wife* who was arriving; draw what he could from them, any further conclusions . . .

With a sardonic twist of his mouth he dismissed it and began reflecting hazily on the circumstances that had landed him in this out-of-the-way hole. His constant money demands of Cecil and Cecil's refusal, always maddeningly calm, smiling and positive; his vengeful departure soon after that with money stolen from his friend—perquisites of that sort he considered his by right. Then his picking up another "friend" who turned out to be a *flic*, of all the shitting luck. On the grey pouring day of his liberation from a brief sojourn in gaol he took with him the memory of the gaol doctor's examining him roughly, contemptuously, along with his consequent distrust and hatred—savage, disproportionate and mindless like all his emotions—of all doctors henceforward. After this the train he had taken in his rage, the first train to anywhere out of rotten filthy Paris; finally this howling wilderness where his ticket had run out; then his state, more and more penniless and more and more frightening . . . and just about this time the old woman he had noticed trying again and again to cross the road, pitiless with its streams of traffic. His indifferent glance at her and his first thought—let her be run over, good riddance—changed as he saw at the throat of her shabby black dress a brooch, a large one. Fake diamonds never blazed like that, also he realised dimly that such design was never seen in junk jewelry. Courteously he offered his help and could still feel, with revulsion, her scared bony clutch on his arm. They crossed the road and continued walking side by side, she burbling her gratitude over and over in a way that began convincing him there was something wrong with her head— though not altogether, not altogether: be careful . . .

Yes, he admitted to her questioning, he was hungry; she invited him home for a meal. From this point he began listening hard to her nonsense, trying to deduce whether she were protected by the presence of a family. Now she was chittering about . . . books, it sounded like books? and shyly, on the chance, he mentioned that he had been thrown out of the University of Paris for participating in student riots. Apparently she missed all of this but the word *university*, screaming in rapture, "Un homme éduqué! Then you can help me! the books, the papers, too heavy . . ."

From this point, always, he entered a territory of fruitless remembrance plus impotent fury, and far from abating with passage of time it grew always more desperately tangled, more maddening. When he found that except for two servants he was alone with her in the chateau, his mind had leaped at once to a quick scoop of jewelry, a getaway . . . which was followed immediately by common-sense rare with him, but gloomy and imperative. He had no way of getting rid of the stuff, no connection with sources of that kind; he was not a criminal, only a parasite, though far from applying any such word to himself. But there it was, jewelry was out . . .

For the time being therefore he had resigned himself to hanging on, learning the ins and outs of the house by heart, while acting as the old woman's beast of burden in the library. That library—! even now the word evoked from him a belch of disgust. To be carrying heavy stuff all day, stacks of crumbling books and papers and all of it thick with dust and stinking of mould; his hands blackened, his back breaking, his clothes being ruined, and all the while one single thought in his head: *In all this there must be something for me, somewhere. In this big place is something, something, if only I can find it.*

A sort of start even now rigidified him as he remembered the day, the moment. He had been emptying by slow degrees a sort of small room or large closet adjoining the library, putting the stuff little by little on the table before which sat the hag. Yes, and her extraordinary intentness (for a crazy one) had struck him even then, but faintly. With a peculiar combination of scattiness accompanied by a desperate concentration she would winnow piles of this trash falling to bits under her violent and clumsy handling, talking to herself al-

ways, soft or loud or medium: "No . . . no . . . not here . . .
not here . . ." Until; until.

He had placed the almost final heap before her, most of
the scrapings off the floor, then from mere exhaustion had sat
down, thinking he would throttle the old *chiot* if she kept
him at this slavery much longer . . . from this swimming fatigue and hatred combined he had been roused by her cry, a
wild exultant sound, strangely powerful coming from a body
so wizened and weak, so old . . .

Yes, and there was the beginning of his troubles, the thing
he had stolen from the table and hidden away . . . With a
furious sound between his clenched teeth he dismissed it and
began thinking vengefully of his hardships and disap-
pointments, his dull parents who had no money, the dull ugly
little town, and everything in him telling him that he was
born for better things than this, *better* . . . then at fifteen
there was the lorry driver bound for the magic name (he had
made sure of this in advance) who had picked him up, a first
admirer whom he had ditched near Paris by excusing himself
to pee and walking off in a direction opposite to the driver's
route. And the fact that he had run into Cecil almost at once
was no consolation, certainly not. Cecil had nothing but an
allowance from England which allowed them one week of
luxury which was fun and three of near-squalor which was
not. And now fate had landed him with this second *anglais*,
this old Dominic, and *he* had no money either, the wife had
it, of all the filthy luck . . . Out of all this one thing remained to him, one strong and invincible thing, which was
his own faith in his physical allure, this faith making up—actually—most of his mentality. Only let him get to a place
where he could show himself to rich men, rich rich men . . .

His mind reverted to the stolen object, which lay on him
heavy as lead from the day he had hidden it. Was it valuable?
Could a thing so ugly, so tattered, be worth *any*thing? He was

sure of only one thing, that the twisted pale writing was not French. But even if it had been in French he would have no idea what it was, he knew nothing of such things, nothing . . . and added to this maddening ignorance was a conviction, somehow greater day by day, that it was *dangerous* to show to anyone, even more dangerous than trying to pawn stolen jewelry. His mind, empty and self-obsessed as it was, also contained instincts like an animal's; intimations of danger shapeless but all the same there, unsleeping and vibrant . . .

Then Dominic: the addition to the scene of Dominic, and his own immediate stirring of giant hope and giant uncertainty, mixed. This man knew about such things, he *knew*, but to risk confiding in him, this soon . . . and before he had made up his mind to take the leap, other vague impediments held him back. Like the vague feeling, for example, that the lover and the professional man were two different people, a warning just now disastrously justified. For all the old one's emotional and sexual subjugation, it was a different matter when it came to his work; he was capable of drawing a hard and fast line over which no one, *no one*, could step. Just see how this professional ascendancy had made him immovable, merciless, only minutes ago; he had imposed his own conditions, he had compelled his adored one into a relationship with his *wife* . . .

A rictus of hatred convulsed the beautiful inhuman face for a moment; his eyes went glassy. He would have to be on terms with this interference, this *woman* . . . he gagged again at the word. Well, be polite for the time being, he had no choice; carry more books and papers like a beast of burden, it would be the same as when the other old bitch was alive. At least his find was safe, no danger of this nasty she-expert getting her claws on it . . .

A memory swept all this away and touched him with annoyance more immediate: his failure to borrow the car. Handy if he could have done so, got to Paris and looked up Cecil, and anyway he yearned for Paris. Only the one single thing, the hidden thing, was keeping him in this miserable *trou* and would continue to keep him here till he had some notion of what to do with it . . . no, he was trapped; there was nothing he could do about it but wait, wait . . .

In the feeling of helplessness, of being squeezed in the giant fist of compulsion, he bared his teeth and stamped violently on the floor. Then at once, ignoring the pain in his foot, he bent again to the spotty mirror and examined himself anxiously, afraid that his paroxysm of fury had left some mark on his face.

VI

"But I'd have been glad to pick you up in Paris," he said, not for the first time. "Glad to."

"You've other things to do here, haven't you?" Be undemanding, be careful, friendly . . . "No, it was easy to fly to Paris and rent a car to here, perfectly easy."

"When did you get here?"

"About an hour ago. I knew—" she forestalled his interruption "—I knew you'd be busy, I didn't want to disturb you."

"How are you, though?" he asked in a tone that—all at once—inspired her with hope; he too sounded . . . friendly? concerned? Yet no use seizing on these favourable signs with starving avidity, not yet; be patient, don't force it . . .

"I'm perfectly all right," she said dismissively. "I was all for driving myself over, but everyone was so against it that I had to give way." A fear that her voice might be trembling (from sickening self-pity) hurried her to another topic. "I've just had visitors."

"Already?" His voice held an entire comprehension.

"They didn't lose a moment. *Some*one must've told them I'd arrived."

"Probably the old girl here, an old servant—they must've tipped her to notify them of arrivals and departures and so

89

forth. And what—" he sounded more alert "—what happened with the two old hags?"

"Screams, yells and idiotic questions." She shrugged. "Apparently they've the wildest hopes from this library of theirs." She shrugged again. "I wouldn't even give an opinion till I'd seen it, which annoyed them—one of them especially."

"Yes, I know which one."

"What a pair," she said over the feeble leap her heart had given; his smile in response to her smile, surely a favourable sign . . . ? "One of them viciously greedy, the other stupidly greedy, and both so suspicious of each other it isn't true. And also—" the new item quickened her voice for a moment "—they're fairly ignorant of their family history. Not altogether, but mostly."

"Yes, I had some such impression the first time I spoke to them.—Now." He became brisk. "Tell me where your luggage is, and I'll carry it to your room."

"Thanks, I've carried it up myself."

"Your*self*—!"

"There wasn't any service laid on, apparently. I didn't bring all that much."

"But of all the stupid—"

"No, no, it's all right." Disproportionately warmed by the continuing appearance of solicitude, she pressed on with more animation than before. "Oh yes, I didn't tell you. One of the old girls, Mme Cotteret, produced their single big gun." Again she smiled. "Their ambassador."

"Oh yes." He reflected. "She told me about that. I shouldn't take the old fool's word for it, myself."

"As it happens she's quite right, they did have one." Merely with the pleasure of being with him, talking to him, she went on with animation, "An ambassador to England."

"What period?"

"1595, '96, something like that."

"Elizabeth!" His own voice quickened a little.

"Yes, but he's of no special interest." She was apologetic. "I crawled out to the BM as soon as I was able, once I had the client's name." She became strenuously off-hand so as not to imply that in research of this kind he, himself, was lazy and indifferent. "I couldn't find out much about him, and nothing very important happened during his embassy. Still, he was the high point of the de Léovils apparently—the great man of the family."

"Still, you might find letters or something." Along with his words something jogged him, of whose source he had no time to think. "Although stuff of that sort—unless there's something completely unexpected you can't do much but present them to some State archive or other."

"I don't believe the sisters intend presenting anything to anybody. Now, would you show me the library?"

"Of course."

"Oh, I forgot to ask you." She closed her mind to the alacrity with which he had got to his feet—alacrity of release. "What do you do about food here? Is there an inn nearby, or anything—?"

"Lord no, nothing like that, we eat here. The heiresses have arranged it with the same old girl that let you in—Mme de Léovil's former maid, I believe." He was holding the door open for her. "Through here." He was silent till they were traversing the first of a series of large gloomy rooms, undoubtedly grand at one time. "By the way, I'd almost forgotten," he put in casually. "I understand there's a librarian of sorts living here. Has anyone told you?"

"Not a word. Oh dear." Her instant forebodings were justified by past experience. In these ancient piles was found, often enough, an equally ancient librarian; some old buffer deeply dug in, especially where the family had no least interest in its old records and never disturbed him in his dusty kingdom—which little by little he came to regard as *his* kingdom, *his* books, *his* documents . . . The attitude of such monarchs, when uprooted, was understandable; hatred against the uprooter, defiance mixed with despair and malice, ready to obstruct in a hundred furtive ways—misinform, pretend ignorance, even hide things . . .

"He's old, I suppose?" she hazarded. "Old as the hills?"

"Actually, I don't think so." Dominic's tone was of a man not even troubling to search his memory. "I think I've seen him at a distance, no one's troubled to introduce him. My impression is that he's young, or fairly young."

"Oh," she murmured. "Well, nothing for it but to wait and see, I suppose."

"Nor and Alex are coming tomorrow, did you know?" he went on quickly, to stand off the threat of a silence; understanding this, she replied dully, "Yes, Uncle Frederick told me." Then her depression lifted in spite of herself; interest and excitement began flickering in her, powerfully, as they approached the high double doors once painted in brown and gold. Whatever her griefs, presumably, and for as long as she could still walk and talk, this anticipation would always stir her. With this release from the grave, and all at once remembering a small curiosity—

"By the way," she pursued. "The side door between our bedrooms—did you know it's locked?"

"Yes, I noticed that." Suddenly going tight, he waited.

"I'm not . . ." She achieved a rusty laugh. "I'm not infectious, you know."

"Of course not," he agreed cordially. "The trouble is, there seems to be no key—there wasn't when I moved in."

"But I'd like it open." She tried to steer a course between uncertainty and pettishness. "We could ask the old woman, couldn't we—"

"We'd better not." He was decisive. "I've been warned

against annoying her unnecessarily, it seems she's a pretty crotchety old . . ." He had opened the right wing of the stately shabby doors, which responded with a shriek and groan combined. "Actually," he added, "I've had a pretty good hunt for the key, and couldn't find it."

On this wretched morning, tightly girded for work and just about to pass through the library doors, she heard vague noises of arrival outside and about-faced at once. Reaching the door that had admitted her to the chateau she ran into a scene of unpacking and unloading, in pouring rain, by the two stalwart elderly men to whom Dominic was lending a hand, and over the clatter of bags and tools and thump of boxes mocked cheerfully, "*Good* morning! Thanks for the lovely weather you've brought!"

"Roight lovely, mum, roight lovely," Alex agreed in a roar; both men had ducked inside, pulled out handkerchiefs and swabbed their faces, while Norbert supplemented, "Reg'lar Bluebeard's castle this would be, mum, eh?"

"Complete with bodies, I shouldn't wonder," she agreed. "Have you had breakfast?"

"Lor' yes, a bite on the plane, then Mr Godfrey he bought us another when he met us." Norbert turned to Dominic. "Shall we get this stuff where it belongs to an' get going, sir? Mr Palgrave, 'e says it's buried treasure loike, eh?"

"Could I see it?" Val put in suddenly. "Just for a moment? Give me some of the smaller stuff, it'll save someone a trip."

In the same cheerful atmosphere of verbal rock-throwing between the workmen they went up and up, all of them heavy-laden, to a region of gloom, thick dust and low ceilings. Alex and Nor had gone back for the rest of their things; the sudden awkwardness of her being alone with Dominic overcome—for the moment—by what was piled up on every side and reached away and away into the murk . . .

93

"Good Lord," she murmured, and Dominic murmured likewise, "There's a good bit of trash mixed in with it."

"Yes, but even so." Unlike her husband, who seemed deliberately to cultivate a sort of blindness in areas outside his own, she possessed a universal and unerring feeling for style, and was staggered by what she saw. A sudden rancour (envy?) prompted her to say ironically, "All this won't hurt you with Uncle Frederick, will it?"

"I hope not," he returned with similar irony, and for a moment her sleeping sense of outrage flared in her with such force that it almost escaped in vituperation, insult . . .

In the end she was going downstairs again to confront the library doors, for the moment without purpose or intention; with nothing in her but the anger and the bitterness, still unspoken.

Having entered she stood still again, perfectly still. The last few moments had revived the souvenir of last night—the mournful bedroom and herself in it alone, the locked door between them and she too stricken by the first sight of the library to protest again, to make any demand on him whatever. She had gone to sleep not only unhappy but profoundly discouraged, and this room was to blame for the discouragement; this enormous room in crazy disorder, books awry on the shelves or tumbled about on the floor and all of it stinking of old dust, old volumes, old everything . . .

"Did he say there was a *librarian?*" she murmured half-aloud, and pressed the switch beside the door. A half-dozen powerful bulbs came to life in the ugly nineteenth-century chandelier; Dominic had not forgotten to replace the single wan bulb of yesterday. By the hard brilliant light, somehow crushingly depressing with the rain outside, she reassessed the bleakness of four high dusty windows and the shelves chaotic or bare, going up to the very high ceiling. A room, like herself, unloved . . .

Angrily she shook this off and considered the territory as yet unexplored, the two doors in a sort of rear niche. On examination one proved to open into a servants' passage, narrow and dark, and the other into a large closet, almost a small room. Already she had made up her mind that if anything of value existed in this wreckage, it would be in the adjoining burrow; but first of all she must deal with the larger area, scrutinise everything in it before indulging unlikely hopes . . . She moved to the nearest shelves, pulled out a few volumes, glanced at them and put them back. Then all at once she realised that she was not fit to climb up to the higher shelves, ordinarily she was a mountain goat but not now, not after an illness. As this inconvenient truth dawned on her she woke belatedly to the sound of a door opening—not the stately entrance but from the side passage—and turned to see someone approaching.

"Good day, madame." He had stopped at a respectful distance, first bowing then remaining in the attitude of a half-bow—a subservience that struck her with the same unpleasant force as his good looks, even beauty one might say, but a beauty . . . inhuman? decadent? or certainly, to her at least, repellent. Also there was the smile pasted on his face, something intended for a smile evidently but having in it no quality of a smile . . . The effect of all this was to wring from her sharply, in fluent French, "Good morning. Are you the librarian?" with a contemptuous accent on *librarian* so that he should not miss it. Nor did he, evidently; a sort of flicker passed across his face without increasing or lessening the smile as he replied, "Ah no, madame, I am no librarian. If someone has called me so—" he shrugged "—it is maybe for a joke."

"Oh." She was slightly taken aback. "Well, are you the . . . the caretaker of this room?"

"No, madame."

"You're not? You've nothing to do with it at all?"

"Nothing at all, madame." With an extra nuance of submissiveness he added, "I was here only with Mme de Léovil, I carried books for her when she wished, and that is all."

So the crazy owner was responsible for the disorder, she thought reasonably, then told him silently and unreasonably, *You might have dusted a bit while you were about it*, then found herself disliking him more from moment to moment; he gave her the creeps somehow, and in addition she guessed —through mere clairvoyance of opposites—at his bone-laziness.

"I came here only when I was told to move books," he had repeated in his soft voice that she thought of, suddenly, as *purring*. "Only then, madame."

"Well." She dismissed it; in this enormous labour that faced her there was no one to help her at all, unless she used this slimy little changeling. While surprised at her own expression, she promised herself to make him work as he had never worked before; she would make him sweat. And if he chose to clear out well and good, she would certainly not stop him, she would manage somehow . . .

"Will you please go and find a good long pair of steps," she ordered briskly, and was happy to see him wince. "And get a good lot of cloths from the kitchen. Then we'll start working hard, because," she added with deliberate malice, "there's a tremendous lot to do."

"That dirty cow!" a scream greeted Dominic the instant he entered the room. "That saleté, that crapaud—" Prancing about half dressed he waved clenched fists, spitting assorted obscenities along with a fine spray of saliva.

Dominic hesitated, but only for a moment. Trouble between his wife and his lover he had anticipated—from the word go—but not quite this abandon of rage. Keeping his tone light he enquired, "What's wrong, then?"

"What is wrong!" It was a full-bodied shriek. "All day she chases me up ladders, the highest ladders to the highest shelves, she makes me bring down books, books, books, there is no end to it! All dirty, all dusty, in two minutes my clothes become filthy, spoiled—"

"Well, I should think you'd have enough sense not to wear your new shirt and jacket."

"But—but—" between strangled eloquence and strangled indignation he seemed ready to burst. "—the first time she s-sees me I must make the good impression, no? How can I tell she will ruin my garments?—And on *purpose!*" he yelled, newly inspired. "She has done it on purpose, this miserable—"

He stopped suddenly, and into the ringing silence threw, in a flat voice, "I will go away. Je m'en vais, c'est tout—" and stopped again, this time with sudden alarm. What if the old one agreed, what if he took him at his word . . . To his immense relief Dominic countered with equal flatness, "Nonsense, you're not going away. Now listen to me."

"No!"

"Listen, I tell you." He suppressed a smile of amusement; the creature half dressed, still grimy from his unwilling labour, was even more beautiful because of his fury. "Come, lie down, I cannot speak to you if you jump about like a flea. Lie down, come. Come, come." He waited till the boy had thrown himself sullenly on the bed, then lay down beside him and addressed the shapely back, not daring to touch it as yet. "You must give me time to arrange our lives. Yours, mine too, very comfortably and pleasantly. We can have a good life together if you help me now. If you blow up, if you run away . . ." His voice failed for a moment. "—who knows what may happen? Where will you go? There is no place nearby for you to stay—"

"Stay?" Maury turned over violently and gave him the benefit of two glaring eyes. "In this dirty village, stay? Thank you! If you think I—"

"See here," Dominic overbore him forcibly. "For the sake of being angry for ten minutes you will spoil everything, how intelligent, no? So be good, be patient." In spite of himself the injunction came out as an entreaty. "Continue helping her, you are being paid for it after all—"

"She has killed me." The faun changed his tune to a snuffle. "My back, she has broken—"

"Nonsense, you're strong as a horse, your muscles have gone soft with laziness." At the scowl that was turned on him he said hastily, "Don't wear any more good clothes in the library, little idiot, and I'll buy you a new jacket and shirt—"

"Three shirts!"

"Very good, three shirts."

Pause: with the clock pressing hard upon him Dominic murmured, "We have so little time together and you waste it like this—"

"Tell me," Maury interrupted unhearingly. "This old stuff she looks at now, it is worth money? much money?"

"Money?" The sudden gambit checked his reaching hand. "How do I know? This is the first day she's looked at them. If she finds anything good she will tell me at supper."

"But—but—a thing written, not printed." His urgency forced him to turn around completely. "This would be valuable?"

"How do you mean?" His impatience made him inattentive, but not completely. "Manuscripts? Have you seen manuscripts?"

"No, no." The faun smiled suddenly, engagingly. "I ask, that is all."

The other, about to continue the delayed caress, paused again. An unclear impression of excitement, hidden or controlled, revived an earlier something, suspicion? a half-suspicion? till he remembered the boy's colossal ignorance . . .

"Do you yourself know," he enquired with utmost politeness, "what you're talking about?"

"No," came meekly. "I am stupid, very stupid."

The innocent disclaimer, false even to Dominic's ear, brought a new and sudden picture to his mind. A Book of Hours? A sixteenth-century masterpiece so beautifully coloured and gilded that this little ignoramus had been induced to steal it . . . ?

"See here," he said abruptly. "If you've pinched anything, and it's valuable, you'll be in trouble from the moment you try to dispose of it. So for God's sake, Maury, if that's it, put it back where you found it. *Don't* risk our lives together, all that happiness, for something worth a few pounds or even a few hundred pounds. Don't, I beg you."

Maury, astonishingly, burst out laughing. "You are funny," he burbled between gusts. "I would make a bad thief, I, but you—you as *prêcheur—*"

"You're laughing, are you?" Dominic said between his teeth. "I'll teach you to laugh, I'll teach you." Curiously, as he took hold of him, a music was evanescently in his mind: a music of murmuring leaves, forest depths, the afternoon of the thing barely seen for a moment, the appearance half-human, half lower god . . .

"I've had callers today," said Val, with a fair imitation of chattiness. "Three guesses."

"The sisterhood?" He had picked up a dish and offered it. "More beans?"

"No thanks.—Yes, they barged in at about three o'clock," she complained. "Just when I was in the thick of it."

"What did they want?"

"What do you suppose?" She laughed mirthlessly. "They wanted me to say I'd found things in the library worth millions."

"And what did you tell them?"

"I gave them chapter and verse—that it's all junk more or less, at least so far."

"So there's nothing good? nothing at all?"

"A certain amount of eighteenth-century stuff." She shrugged. "In fair to poor condition. *Le Grand Cyrus* and so forth, nothing earlier. Tons of nineteenth-century trash—it's all hardly worth sending even to a local auctioneer."

"I see." He frowned. "It's all a waste of your time, then?"

"Well, I haven't finished, something good might come up. You can revive me with a bucket of water, if so." She smiled. "The old girls went off harbouring the deepest suspicions of my honesty, you could tell."

The topic was finished, one of those silences he feared had set in. Along with this he was aware of something less definable in his mind—a confused dissatisfaction, uneasiness . . . ? Still, she knew what she was talking about if anyone did . . .

By now the old woman had brought in the coffee grudgingly, as she did everything; his wife began pouring. With a murmured thanks he accepted a cup from her hand, put in sugar, then sat stirring and stirring, while various recognitions caught up with him. He was tired, tired, he had had a strenuous day helping the two cabinet makers while listening to their pungent comments on their village lodging, food, landlady, all with dirtiest good humour. By tomorrow they would have a quantity of stuff boxed and ready to go, say half the first lorry-load; he had already laid on vans, insurance, everything. Then on top of this first fatigue was the later fatigue, he could still feel it in all his limbs, a delicious enervation all though him . . .

". . . the so-called librarian." Her voice brought him out of his languor with a shock; he had missed the beginning of her sentence altogether, and now she sat waiting for his answer . . .

"What about him?" he managed indifferently.

"Nasty." She was brief and decisive. "He gives me the horrors. And *lazy*—!"

"Oh?" His problem, now, was to conceal his extreme watchfulness. "Any use to you, though?"

"In spite of himself." She laughed briefly. "Not by his own will, I promise you. And am I making him *move*—up the ladder, down the ladder—!"

"Well, then he *is* of some use."

"Oh yes, I suppose so. I can't go skimming up to the high shelves, not yet." She stirred her coffee absently. "But I feel that this little rat's getting ready to turn on me in some way, he hates me murderously—this soon." She lifted the cup and sipped. "Black looks, you never saw the like.—Dominic." Her voice changed. "Couldn't you find me someone else to help, just for carrying books? Couldn't you . . . ?"

"I'm afraid not, in this neighbourhood. I needed someone myself, earlier on, but absolutely nothing doing." He had prepared the lie about needing help in advance, but the paucity of local labour was no lie. "There're farmers' people, all busy, and beside that a lot of old men—you see them sitting about, inside and outside a sort of village estaminet."

"Oh." It was a sound of acceptance; she was silent for another moment, then asked, "Is it all right if I use the phone, here? I don't like to bother you for transport, and I'm afraid I can't walk to the village, not yet."

"I should think it would be all right. Keep track of your calls and I'll settle up when we go."

She nodded, then made her own mistake—of letting the silence stretch out, take hold, every moment that passed making it more and more difficult to break . . . She glanced at him with sudden irrational hope, and at once he produced the yawn he was holding in readiness, stifled it with his hand and murmured, "Excuse me."

"Tired?" she asked, at once thrown back on herself.

"More than tired." Artistically he killed another yawn. "Whacked." Without seeming to he watched her carefully, entirely comprehending her state of mind. She wanted to come to his room, perhaps only to lie beside him and for a little while be held . . . only a faint twitch of the nose betrayed his interior grimace. From the very first of their marriage that desire of hers, *to be held*, had irritated him increasingly. And this desire was evident to him now, it was as loud as if spoken and he must not give her the chance to speak it, he must not . . .

"I'm turning in." He got up decisively. "Sorry, but I can hardly keep my eyes open."

"All right." She had said it after an imperceptible pause that let him get as far as the door. Once there, with an access of something unclear to himself—shame? embarrassment? he turned and asked, "You'll be all right?"

"Oh yes, thank you," she answered. "Perfectly all right."

A little later she was in bed, suddenly plowed with fatigue but as suddenly wide awake; refusing to admit to herself why she was not asleep, why she was fighting off sleep . . . She heard it at last, the reason why not: the sounds from next door, stealthy and hardly perceptible, all but not there, yet furiously plain to her furious wide-awake anguish. *She's here*, she thought with a stab of comprehension. *He's brought her along, he's got her here somewhere, hidden somewhere* . . .

Then all at once the bright scourging misery turned everything black, and the blackness flooded in and drowned her.

Rain made a silence. Or made a silence ordinarily; this morning it was broken by varied and continuous racket.

Seated at the phone, two rooms away from the stately entrance hall but with the doors open between, absently she listened to the grunts, jocular abuse, and irregular footsteps
under heavy loads; the first installment of massive packing-
cases was being carried downstairs. Dominic's voice, incisive,
was distinct among the workmen's, and all at once—by this
grey, factual daylight—it seemed to her that her last night's
certainty had been wrong, wrong to the point of craziness; did
her husband's manner and appearance this morning, his crisp
and total devotion to the job, tie up with a night of passionate dalliance? All nonsense more likely, the workings of the
imagination made sinister by night . . . *The power of darkness*, she thought with a half-smile, then became alert as London and then Palgrave's answered.

"Val! how are you? how are you?"

"All right, dear, I'm—"

"You're sure? it's not too much for you?"

"No, no, I'm fine. But Uncle Frederick, I'm afraid it's not
very good news."

"Oh." Instantly silenced, he paused a moment. "Carry on."

"The library's a complete zero, in wild disorder to boot, just
a big room full of muck. And what isn't absolute muck, a few
eighteenth-century novels and religious works, might fetch
something moderate at a secondhand dealer's, given time."

"M'hm," he grunted after a moment. "And that's the lot,
is it?"

"So far it's the lot. There's a sort of secondary room adjoining the library, more of a closet actually, simply crammed
with stuff—not books, it looks like old papers of some sort.
But more on the floor than on the shelves, a perfect rat's-nest
—I haven't started on any of it yet."

"Well." His voice hung between faint hope and strong
dubiousness. "You never know what'll turn up in stuff of that
sort."

"No, but don't expect too much," she warned affection-
ately. "This isn't a family full of famous people, there's nothing distinguished but one ambassador, long long ago."

"How long?"

"The Virgin Queen."

"Well! you might find something there."

"I'm afraid it's too late in the reign," she apologised.
"About 1595 on, and she was getting pretty old, losing her
health—still," she concluded, "I don't propose to miss anything, not one single thing."

"Dig up a king's whore, couldn't you?"

"I'd love to," she assured him. "But even if I did, what are
those ladies worth at auction?"

"Damned little." He was gloomy again. "It sounds as if
you'd better tell the heirs to get rid of them as they like."

"We'll see." She disliked leaving him in this dank mood,
but no help for it. "Bye-bye then, I'll let you know if anything
turns up."

There was no answer at all; against the sudden silence she
persisted, "Uncle Frederick . . . ?"

"It's all right, my love, it's only James just come in."

"Give him my best, will you?"

"James, Val says give you her best." Without pausing he
harked back. "Have you seen the furniture that Nor and Alex
are working on?"

"Just a glimpse. You're going to make a noise with this, a
tremendous noise."

"That's what your husband says, and I've never found him
very far out."

Having rung off and regarded his nephew who stood waiting with papers in his hand, he said without pause and sourly,
"Why in hell didn't you marry her?"

"I'd have liked to," the younger man replied, imperturbable in the face of this unexpected dart. "I asked her once, actually."

"Did you, by Jove! You never told me."

"No."

"But what happened?"

"She was very . . . courteous." A hint of smile, bleak, crossed his face. "Asked for a while to think about it. And just about then, you engaged Dominic." The faint smile, once more, appeared and disappeared. "She fell like a ton of bricks —couldn't marry him fast enough."

The elder Palgrave started to say, *I've never really liked that chap somehow,* stopped himself with annoyance—he hated unfairness, above all to an employee as expert as Dominic—and employed his half-open mouth with a different sentiment. "A bit of bad luck, but it needn't keep you from trying elsewhere."

"I might do that, one day." James was unshakably polite. "Now here's the final stuff for the Cloverley sale, the jewelry, silver plate, and James I miniatures."

"Thanks." Absently accepting the papers the elder Palgrave said, absently, "According to Val the library there's a wash-out."

"Yes? but something might turn up—?"

"Not according to the signs, so far."

"Well, she knows."

"You bet she knows."

Maury, in the silent bedroom that had belonged to the dead woman, waited till the others had rung off before replacing the phone with infinite gentleness. About to relapse into thought he reminded himself that someone *might* come up here, someone *might* see him emerging from where he had no business to be; he must go elsewhere . . . Eeling out with caution, closing the door behind him and starting for his own room, he changed his mind instantly and with annoyance. He needed somewhere to think, and how to do this when Dominic had the habit of coming in unexpectedly in hopes of dalliance . . . The old boy had it badly, he thought with complacence, but first things came first . . .

In one of the countless half-dark servants' passages behind the rooms he settled himself on a step, and for the thousandth time flung himself against his particular and insoluble problem. Unfortunately for him this calculation, in view of his mental quality and general experience, seemed likely to do him as little good in the end as in the beginning. Again he saw himself with the old woman in the library, again he was bringing load after load of trash from the closet and laying it before her; again he heard her ancient voice raised in the screech of joy, a penetrating screech like some crazy old machine . . .

More vivid than anything else though, more exquisitely transfixing, was his memory of the next few moments. Her excitement, her wild quivering transport, her short breathing and small wordless cries as she seemed hardly to dare touch it, then with the same fear ventured to turn a page gently, prepared to turn another . . .

And even as his bored and secretly derisive eyes had flicked away from her and returned, already she was crumbling under the stroke, her eyes gone witless, her mouth half open. And he could pride himself, he was still priding himself, on what had followed. Far from raising the alarm he had bent over her, with one negligent hand keeping her from sliding off the chair, and taken a first look at what she had been examining. Not a book but a lump of pages fastened together like a book with cord almost perished; old and tattered, ugly enough to make you throw up, the faintest writing in some language certainly not French. A little like English maybe? but who could read such stuff, it tired him even to think of it . . .

Yet on sudden impulse, devoid of intelligence like all his impulses, he had done two things: first of all cleared the table before her of its upheaval of papers, taken them back to the closet, and buried them under the remnant still lying at the bottom from no more cause than a directionless instinct of secrecy. While in the closet, he had heard the faint *crump* that meant she had fallen out of her chair; he did not even look to see. When he came out there she was, all right, lying on the floor. Ignoring her, once more he bent over the scrattle of pages that had so excited her; finally taking it up and forcing it—with an accompanying shower of dry broken-off bits—into a pocket. The thing was old, that much was certain, old things might be valuable . . . on this thought he left the room at a leisurely gait, substituting for it the agitated voice and step of disaster only when he neared the kitchen.

From this past scenario, invariable, he returned to his present indecisions, and the more he circled around them the worse they got. His constant conjecture on his hidden trove, his further examinations, failed to enlighten him. On the remnant of top page, which had suffered especially from being crammed into the pocket, was the beginning of something in large writing but broken off after a word or two, he could hardly distinguish a letter of it. Yet it was *old*; to this belief he clung stubbornly, old things could be worth a fortune. But offer it how? where? and with Dominic's unpleasant warning stubbornly in his ears? If the thing were really valuable he would have the cops on his neck in two seconds, an experience he had no desire to invite . . . he groaned aloud while thrusting the object back into an old magazine and replacing it beneath a pile of others. He must have advice, he must, there were people who knew about such things. But it was dangerous to ask here, he must get out of this hole, this God-forsaken dump . . .

Without realisation he was already on his feet, the resolution that brought him upright carving his face, his manner, everything about him, to implacable purpose.

"But what for? Why do you want a car?"

"I want it, c'est tout." With haughty disdain he stared at Dominic. "You said I could rent one if I desired it. You said so—!"

"All right, all right. Where—" Over a sudden curious failing of the heart he asked with false jocularity "—where do you want to go?"

"To Paris. In a bank," he improvised fluently, "there will be a little money that comes to me, I cannot let it lie there."

You could have them send it, was on the tip of Dominic's tongue and as quickly withdrawn. Instead, he ventured, "Take the train."

"No!" The flash of temper was all the more vicious for his having divined the fear—almost grovelling fear—that had prompted the suggestion. "I will not exhaust myself getting to the train and getting back, that bitch of yours has already crippled me enough. Anyway, you promised me—!"

"All right, all right." His timidity and subservience were turning him slightly sick. "How do I know," he asked, again humorously, "if you'll come back?"

"But certainly I will come back." The faun's wide and candid eyes expressed his deep hurt. "How can you think I will not come?"

"And how much," Dominic countered, "do you think you'll need?" and at the answer said involuntarily, "Oh Lord!" and reflected for an instant. The funds he had at his disposal were the firm's; of his own he had brought along very little and merely in case, not having in the least anticipated the turn of events. There appeared to be only one resource, nothing else for it . . . "Wait a moment," he said curtly, and hurried downstairs. "Val?" he called, entering the library, then saw she was not there—

"Dominic?" Her voice came from behind him; he turned and saw her dimly inside the recess. "Not a vestige of light in this hole," she said, her heart beginning to hammer suddenly; she waved an electric torch. "Perfectly maddening."

"I expect so." He pitched his voice to careful lack of urgency. "Val, can you let me have some money?"

"Of course." An impasse of thought—part from fatigue and discomfort, part from undefined let-down—somehow blanked out her least query about the demand. "How much?"

"A thousand francs or so?"

"Take it, will you? traveller's cheques in the zipped compartment." With blackened hands she indicated her handbag. "I don't want to touch it."

"You'll have to sign them," he reminded her.

"Oh damn! Bring them here, would you, with my pen?"

"Here's mine."

"Thanks."

He stood while she wrote her name over and over, said with businesslike brusqueness, "Thank you," then carefully restored the cheque-book to its place in the handbag, like a proper husband.

Only when Maury had seized the beautiful objects from him and was retreating in a hurry with his loot—

"Have you given her notice about this?" Dominic asked suddenly; it had not occurred to him before. "Have you told her?"

"No," the faun smiled tranquilly. "You will tell her."

He vanished.

VII

Under the harsh pitiless overhead light she sat engaged in her first essay at the closet; the tableful of papers must be sorted and sorted before even one of these dusty sheets, whether whole or fragmented, could be examined. However, as is the case with most old papers, their separate characters became evident in a little while. Stewards' accounts in fairly good condition; expenses of the house for servants, food, furniture, hangings, stuffing for beds and pillows; provision for entertainments, including one tremendous affair graced by the presence of Louis XIV, which left the establishment virtually bankrupt for months; stable accounts, the carriages, the resident blacksmith, all going backward from the eighteenth century.

As she dived deeper, her irritation at having to carry armfuls of papers from the closet was submerged in the fascination of this domestic machinery; a passionate antiquarian, she could have wasted any amount of time on records of visits, illnesses, lyings-in, fees for the physicians, the midwives . . . unfortunately, no time for such deliciousness. Toward six o'clock she stopped, exhausted and filthy, with no room in her mind for anything but a hot bath and a lie-down before dinner, a long one . . .

Wonderful, how she had revived after only a short rest; it

must be a sign that she was recovering, genuinely. Her appetite was coming back too, a loss much older than her loss of strength; unhappiness had killed all desire for food even before her illness set in. But now she was hungry, wildly hungry for the first time in weeks. Eating with this new enjoyment she responded to Dominic's essays at conversation too animatedly, somehow buoyed with a hope—unreasoning, springing from this revival of her body—that perhaps it might be all right after all, perhaps his willingness to talk was a forerunner of reconciliation, a preparation for saying he was sorry, then everything would be all right again . . .

Poor thing, Dominic reflected meanwhile, *poor bitch,* all the various sources of her vivacity plain to him as red lights. *How in hell am I going to handle this, she's working up to something.* As she rattled on about what she had found in the library closet—*Female,* he was thinking with gloomy distaste. *Must be a female thing, that inability to accept that a man's through with them,* then tried to remember if he had ever encountered this complication when parting with a man. Maybe, he concluded at last, but not in the same way as with a woman, not with such scenes, disgusting and violent . . . His experience with women was almost non-existent, apart from his marriage. All the same, instinct somehow warned him: this woman with her comely face pale with recent illness, her neat little figure and immaculate good breeding, her gentle voice and oddly studious nature, was capable of raising hell. How or when he did not know, but his premonition was more and more insistent . . .

"Sorry," he said abruptly. "What was that?"

At once she was taken aback, staring at him with that *asking* look that gripped him, as always, with distaste.

"Frightfully sorry," he pursued. "I suddenly thought of something I'd forgotten about . . ." he gestured upward.

"If I'm boring you," she began with sudden timidity.

For Christ's sake don't go pathetic, he snarled silently while replying, "Lord no, I'm interested." He had missed every word of hers for the last couple of minutes, and skilfully retrieved the position by asking a question always safe, in their particular profession. "How long at it will you be, d'you think?"

"I don't know, actually. Everything runs backward from 1793." This allusion to the French Revolution also exerted its curious power—of making a pause. "Everything in this hidey-hole," she continued, "is just slung on top of everything else."

"So the deeper down you go," he enquired, "the earlier the dates?"

"So far, yes, but it's all such a mess that I'm not sure of anything. What's lower down," she shrugged, "is anyone's guess."

"No personal letters?" He had to say something. "Nothing like that?"

"Not yet. Some fascinating account books, I'm down to about 1680—Oh!"

Her sudden breaking off made him quail and go rigid at once; he knew what she was going to say.

"By the way, that miserable little chap's walked out on me, simply quit without saying a word. Not a word, mind you!"

"Is that so." His appearance of surprise was masterly, not too much nor too little. He had balked at obeying Maury's casual injunction to "tell her": let the little bastard tell her himself.

"Still," she was continuing, "it's what I'd expect, from that type."

"Well, you did say," he reminded her, "that he was pretty much useless to you—?"

"I didn't exactly. Or did I?" She reflected. "What I meant was that he's certainly no librarian, he admitted it himself, but he's useful for carrying stuff that's heavy."

"But how have you managed?" His quick response was impelled by one single, sudden fear. Let her over-exert herself so soon, let her fall ill again in this place, what a mess . . . "How did you work it today?"

"How d'you think? It didn't carry itself."

"Now see here," he said with authority. "No more of that, d'you hear? No more carrying heavy stuff, you'll be falling on your face next thing. From now on I'll put on your table whatever you want for the day's work, and if you need anything else, come and tell me. Now remember!" he commanded. "Remember!"

"I'll remember," she said meekly, but obviously—too obviously—pleased by his solicitude. Both symptoms alarmed him all over again, yet what could he have done but make the offer, what in hell else . . . ?

"What's that?" he said with unintended harshness; again he had missed something. "What did you say?"

"I only said, the fairy prince won't come back." She was evidently surprised by his tone. "Why, what's the matter?"

"Nothing, just . . . something else . . ." He gestured vaguely while wondering: had she meant anything by that *fairy* prince, had she . . .

"Yes," she resumed her own train of thought. "I'm pretty sure I've seen the last of the sprite."

She had meant nothing at all, he perceived with relief, then remembered that sly or covert meanings were never her way, that she was much more likely to come out plump with truth however hazardous, a habit that had irritated him frequently. She was unworldly, her inheritance perhaps from a distinguished but eccentric father, of whom she had told him various tales . . . Yes! he thought suddenly, finding a word for her quality; it was a sort of innocence, destructive innocence . . .

"Let's take this," broke in upon him, "and go somewhere else."

She was standing, the coffee-tray in her hands; he had not the least remembrance of when it had come in.

"Couldn't we have a little fire, it's a bit chilly this evening?" she was saying. "All those vast empty fireplaces, and no fire?"

"But didn't they mention it—?"

"Who, the grim sisters? what?"

"That the fireplaces can't be used. A blaze started from one of them just before I came, apparently, the stink was still in evidence. They never told you?"

"No, they must have forgotten. Well, let's find a window, a nice big one—view the scenery." She moved ahead, carrying the tray; wordless, reluctant, watchful and angry, he followed.

"Here's a nice place." Having wandered into one of the reception rooms full of musty silence, musty grandeur and immense windows giving on a neglected terrace, she suggested hopefully, "It would be lovely to sit out there."

"Sit on what?" he asked briefly.

"There's a bench."

"I don't much fancy cold marble under me on an evening as cool as this. Anyway, the bench looks like falling to bits."

"You're right, of course. Well, let's sit here."

They arranged themselves on two vast armchairs in a window embrasure; he pulled over a tabouret for the coffee. When they had their cups they sat sipping and regarding the first signs of autumn outside in silence, at first a perfectly acceptable silence which became—as is the habit of silences —perilous, stuffed with imminence, finally near to desperate . . .

Darling, darling Dominic, she entreated silently, *say something please, say anything*, and sighed.

"Tired?" he asked at once, out of an equal desperation.

"A little." Her sigh had not been of weariness but of impasse; they were back again to fake conversation. "This sort of job."

"Lord yes, unproductive—I know."

"How're you going along upstairs?" she laboured on. "You and the lads?"

"Oh, great guns. They know what they're doing, at all times."

"Oh yes. Yes, of course." Her mind had wandered away from the second emptiness that fell. "I'm so glad to be up and doing again." There, that was a gambit he could hardly receive in silence. "I was so sick of that bed—!"

"I can imagine."

"That *empty* bed," she blurted, then sat scared at what she had not intended. Yet it was done, now she had to go on. "Terribly empty."

"Well." His laugh was forced. "You wouldn't have wanted company in a sick-bed."

"No, maybe not. But now . . ." She paused; for all his failure to take advantage of the pause, she had to rush on, "Oh Dominic, I missed you. I missed you *so*—!"

He muttered something—indistinguishable as it happened, but it made no difference; nothing could stem what now came tumbling out pell-mell.

"I was lonely, lonely, I never felt anything like it before. Like death, really it was, really, I can't tell you . . . as if everything had *stopped*, the world, everything—as if—as if—" Remotely she knew she had made a mistake, she was doing it the wrong way at the wrong time, but to break off now was beyond her power. "Oh Dominic, tonight—I mean, before I—before I go to sleep couldn't I—couldn't I just come in your room . . . I mean, just lie beside you a little while and . . . and have you hold me. It's all I want," she repeated dementedly. "It's all I want, just to be held."

His wordlessness might have warned, but nothing could hold her now from rushing upon her destruction.

"Will you, Dominic?" she wound up feverishly. "Will you, I mean . . . may I—?"

"Val," he groaned, half-audibly. "Val, for God's sake."

On both of them a stillness fell for a moment, stillness with everything in it immobilised: breath, movement, thought . . .

"All right," she mumbled without knowing it, then all at once—"All right!" she shrieked, her voice no longer recognisable. "All right, don't, sorry I asked, very sorry—shan't do it again—" She caught her breath and smiled, a frightening smile. "Go on, *be* faithful to her, you think I don't know you've got her here, somewhere? You think I haven't heard you sneaking out of your room to go to her—discreetly, oh so discreetly?" Her laugh was savage. "B-but one thing I'll tell you, my love, one s-single thing." Her voice fell lower, her smile became still more hateful. "No divorce. Don't plan to marry your s-slut because no divorce, before I give you one I'll die, I'll die first . . ."

Divorce, he echoed silently, then with astonishment thought, *why divorce?* Along with confusion at this sudden change in his sentiments, was wonderment at his foolishness. *I don't want it*, he continued wordlessly, *divorce isn't necessary.*

Meanwhile she had gone quiet again, with dull eyes and vacant face of exhaustion; he sat equally still in a protective blankness except for the indistinct thought, *What now, what next . . .*

"I think I'll go to bed." Her voice was dry and tired; she had risen and moved toward the door before pausing again. "You'd better take that back to the dining-room, she's not likely to come after it." She indicated the coffee-tray. "Good night."

Cecil was not only still in his old haunts, an upstairs room in a shabby house, he was even at home; a great piece of luck which gave the visitor a vague feeling of good omen, of everything continuing to go smoothly. He looked—as always, whatever hole he emerged from—clean, smart, carefully dressed, prosperous-looking; a gift peculiarly English, *l'air anglais* the caller thought, also encouraged by the fact that he received Maury as if he had last seen him yesterday.

"Well, how have you been getting along?" was his first cheerful and unsurprised enquiry. No questions with it, no *where, how* or *why*, not a word of reference to the quarrel which had broken them up, no inconvenient curiosity of any sort; now this was the *comfortable* way of getting along with a friend. More and more he had begun to tire not only of the constricting nature of Dominic's affection but to sense the other potential in it, the potential bondage—of extreme jealousy. And unless it were very much worth his while he would not put up with jealousy, mon dieu, one might as well live in a cage . . .

"Sess-eel," he plunged without preliminary, "j'ai besoin de tes conseils."

"Advice unlimited, my old," drawled Cecil. "Fire away."

"You are educated," the other drove on feverishly. "You have been in the big English universities—"

"I? come off it." Languidly Cecil disclaimed the honour. "Six months of Cambridge did for me, chum, je suis père et mère des illettrés."

"No, no, but listen, you would—you would know about—"

He stopped dead, and his manner of stopping roused in Cecil—for the first time—not his curiosity, for he was abnormally incurious, but a first flickering of concern. Had the little fool got himself into a mess of some sort? It began to sound that way . . .

"Or rather," he amended his disclaimer, "what is it that I'd know about?"

"Well . . . books! or—or maybe not books, not précisement . . ."

At the second full stop Cecil's glance had wandered afield for an instant before returning to him; the slightest frown twitched between his eyes as he enquired gently, "Not a book?" For an instant (being by no means the illiterate he had claimed) he had visions of fifteenth-century manuscripts, hand-lettered texts, gilded capitals, illuminations . . . things of that sort did surface from time to time. "Or would you mean a . . . manuscript?"

The other's faint jerk, start, whatever it was, provided Cecil not only with further puzzlement, but even the beginnings of apprehension. His intelligence, completely first-class, was eroded by a laziness amounting to pathological, but all the same his feeling for the little idiot—call it protectiveness however languid—brought various images to his mind. Long since he had sized him up; nothing to him but that beautiful face and body, a greed perfectly ruthless but mindless; in a word no mind at all, a potential petty criminal but stupid, fatally *stupid* . . . more and more strongly he felt that the boy was rushing upon disaster of some sort, serious trouble involving the police. Yet no use questioning him direct, he would dry up; look at him now, waiting with anxious haunted eyes, his beautiful mouth half-open . . .

"*Is* it a manuscript?" he continued probing gently with apparent indifference. "With big coloured letters? gilded?"

"No!" The monosyllable cut him short. "No! it is . . . it is pages, dirty, torn, with—with writing—" His manner of stopping, again explosive, simultaneously confirmed not only the other's first suspicions, but provided him with a set of new ones. His conviction, now, was that the boy had been picked up by some wealthy old or elderly man, some connoisseur of books; from the library of this man he had stolen something or other, yet to ask him, *Where did you get this thing in the first place?* would not only dry him up completely, but very likely drive him away altogether. Nor did Cecil have any desire to drive him away, he was beginning to feel some agreeable stirrings. Yet before indulging them, and against his will almost . . .

"See here," he began. "You won't say what you've got hold of, all right, I'm not asking you, actually I don't want to know. But one thing I'll tell you: if you've pinched the thing from some collection somewhere, and try selling it, the cops'll have you within a day or two, and it won't go well with you. It might be famous, whatever you've taken, and bibliophiles—" he simplified "—book-experts all over the world will know what it is and whom it belongs to—" He broke off as something else occurred to him. "Is it in French?"

Maury's sullenness, deepening from the first word of the homily, lifted for a moment. "I do not know," he mumbled. "It is a—a writing pale, very pale, I cannot read . . ."

Latin, Italian or Spanish, Cecil diagnosed rapidly, and continued, "Well, all I wanted to tell you was that, and I'll repeat it: if you try selling it you'll be up to your neck in trouble, and at once. Put it back for God's sake, put it back before the owner realises it's gone."

This virtual echo of Dominic's words reduced the other to helplessness, then to smouldering rage; after a moment he began, slowly, getting to his feet.

"What now?" asked Cecil, negligent and unmoving. "Where are you going?"

"None of your affair, I will ask someone who is not—not *stupid* like you—" On the poisonous inflection of *stupid* he broke off as a new, dazzling possibility occurred to him. "Listen, Sess-eel, listen. Do you not know of . . . of someone who . . . who buys such things, secretly—"

"A fence?" A shout of laughter exploded from Cecil. "Dear child, I'm no criminal with criminal connections, I'm merely a remittance man.—Come now, come." The other's look of defeat and childish disappointment had softened him at once. "Don't go away like this, please don't, Maurice-George. Do you have to be back soon—wherever you've come from—?"

"No, I do not have to be back," snarled Maury, reassembling some fragments of his wounded pride. "I am not a shopkeeper's boy."

"And who said you were? Don't be an ass. What I wanted to say . . ." he ventured the edge of a smile ". . . my allowance has just come. Why not stay all night, we'll go and have dinner at the Tour d'Argent, h'm?" His voice was beguiling. "And I promise you absolutely I shan't say another word about this thing, it's your affair, tomorrow you can make more enquiries or whatever you like. Well?" Smiling more broadly he came nearer and touched Maury's cheek, speaking much lower. "What d'you say?"

VIII

Divorce. The word had not only accompanied him to bed, it had haunted his sleep and was all but on his tongue as he awoke. *Divorce, divorce.* But now that she had thrown it in his face in whatever connection—she would give it, she would not give it—he found a whole new idea dawning upon him, a new and eminently sensible possibility. Such things could be arranged, he had seen them arranged—and in a manner that disposed entirely of legal interference, always undesirable . . .

Yet, now that he had the idea more or less formulated, he woke to an unforeseen obstacle—that he had never considered the second party to the arrangement, and therefore knew absolutely nothing about the likelihood of her acceptance or rejection. From the first she had represented to him both an easier life and a quicker prospect of success. Now, with his most recent memory of her as she sat across from him at table —her frozen look, her silence—he knew he must get down to those aspects of their life together which he had never considered *fully*; no, not even for a moment . . .

First of all there was the nature of their relationship, and the quality of that relationship was due (perhaps) less to his own failure than to her lack, her *complete* lack, of endowment. Furthermore, the question of acquiring a little more expertise had probably never occurred to her . . . yes! if any blame were to be apportioned, she had to carry her share. At once he felt an easing and lightening in himself at this conclusion, then proceeded cautiously as if driving on a bad road. Well, if he were right so far, his idea looked like becoming more and more viable. As for her reception of the proposal he was going to make, she had naturally a very even equable temper . . .

Here his progress received a jolt; he saw again her furious eyes and distorted face, heard the furious vindictiveness in her voice. But that had been most extraordinary, quite outside of his usual experience of her; a momentary thing, it would probably never happen again. (As it happened he was quite right, it never did.)

Now his mind began to touch uneasily on her—misunderstanding, misconception, whatever it was—of his own position in the matter. Out of her unworldliness had come the idea that his withdrawal from her bed was because of another woman. And for God's sake let her go on thinking so, for the present at least; if she had any inkling at all of the truth . . .

His involuntary quailing not only brought him up short but forced him to look, and look unsparingly, at all the probabilities. If she found out about him prematurely, above all in combination with the object of his affections (here he quailed again) there was no telling what might happen . . . except of course that he knew what would happen. She would be revolted, horrified, she would not lose a moment in getting rid of him. Worse, she would see that he lost his job, she would go straight to old Palgrave with the tale; her natural generosity would never work in this instance, it was too much to hope for . . .

In the end, and for the present, he settled to a convinced but indeterminate line of thought. At present do nothing, nothing at all. Her rejection of divorce was all right, it suited him excellently. For the rest simply wait, wait and see . . .

His mind touched unwillingly on the day he had spent with her after that ugly scene and fled at once, fled from the memory; source of his instant belch, and no wonder. Stop thinking of it, let the sleeping dog lie. He himself might as well go to sleep, it was hardly daybreak outside . . .

In fact the two of them, at this juncture, were victims of error both surface and underground, almost too subtle to define and harder still to express. His mistake (realised later) was mere incomprehension of character, having in itself unavoidable results. Her mistake (never realised then nor later) was to have had her body betray her; to have had without knowing it—when she petitioned to come to his bed—the first real stirring of desire for her husband.

In the filthiest of tempers Maury, having exhausted every recourse that he could think of, was returning to the chateau. His rhythmic recurrence of rage prompted him to drive deliberately through every sloppy place on the road, and the sloppier the better. The heavier churning of the wheels, the liquid mud flying up torrentially and landing on the car with a *splat!* gave him a pleasure savage and vengeful, but hardly consoling. Even the thought of the last two days, full of pleasures and luxuries, was inadequate to soothe him in the face of his later experiences in Paris. Following his friend's few and unwilling suggestions (Cecil had no idea of getting involved in anything suspicious) he had visited three booksellers and a couple of public libraries, and still ground his teeth at the thought of his reception in those places.

The bookshops chosen by Cecil, a buyer of more books than he could afford, were places whose apparent shabbiness and obscurity belied both their lists of collectors and the flourishing business they did. In all of them he had insisted on speaking with the proprietor (inconveniently in all cases as it happened) and then proceeded to clumsy questions, veiled hints, a constant evasiveness when driven into a corner by questions progressively more determined as to just *what* was he talking about? What, if anything, had he to sell? And after this his dismissal from all of them, being thrown out bodily could not have been fuller of contempt—also of suspicion, though this he had not recognised. All three men had put him down, accurately, as a thief who had got his hands on something he was too ignorant to evaluate or even describe; all three, likewise, had heaved regretful sighs on the loss (perhaps) of a great bargain, along with the impossibility of doing business with such a type.

In the libraries, too, it had been no better. Without the knowledge to ask for the chief librarian he had haunted the circulation desks, plaguing the minor librarians with questions vague, portentous, leading nowhere . . . in one case, even, the attention of the senior librarian was drawn to his activities; a severe elderly woman had approached, said that she had been observing him for the past quarter hour, asked for his reader's ticket, then summarily invited him to leave. Even the thought of what he would like to do to this dried-up stately old besom with her clipped voice and her spectacles, failed to satisfy him . . .

At this point his mind returned, with a new and vague unease, to the chateau. To Dominic he gave not a thought; he would be angry at his overstaying and at the garage's complaint on the car's condition; let him be angry. No, it was the woman who disturbed him now; the *wife*, the bitch with her pale skin, her pale-brown hair, above all her cool manner and her composure; anyone else's composure always became, somehow, an insult to himself . . . all at once the cause of his uneasiness blazed up in him like a forest fire. By now she must have come to the closet with its masses of papers on the floor, yes, she must have. Had she come, yet, to what he had stowed underneath them? Which reminded him, cataclysmically, that he had not even looked at what he had buried, to save his life he would not know it if he saw it . . . Or suppose she had found it already, would it give her any line to what he had pinched? He had stayed away too long, that was the size of it; he had absented himself at the wrong time, just at the wrong time . . .

His small sound of anguish was followed by an icy resolution. He would offer apologies, tell her a tale, then she would let him help her again. She would let him because he *willed* it so, it was necessary for him and therefore she would agree. Surely she could not have reached the bottom of the accumulation, not yet. He would find it first, destroy it before it told her what it had told the old dead one, whatever this information had been. He began assuring himself that he would know it if he saw it, surely he would know it . . .

Without realising he had arrived at the village; in a couple of minutes he had driven into the garage, coolly referred the angry proprietor to Dominic, and walked out. His gait, as he slogged back to the chateau, was uncharacteristically quick and determined. Find the hag, blandish her with a tale if she were angry at his defection, find out casually how far down she had got in the closet; find out by any or all means, find out, find out . . .

"Uncle Frederick?"

"Well! and how are you, lass?"

"Perfectly all right, thanks—"

"You're sure?" he cut her off. "Sure you're not overdoing?"

"No, no, absolutely not. I just wanted you to know how it's going, so far."

"Yes?" Abruptly his interest displaced his solicitude. "Yes—?"

"There's nothing new about the books, I'm afraid, you can count them out definitely. Now this closet I told you about, full of papers—"

"Anything good?"

"Not so far." Almost she could see his face. "For a family that old I'd have expected more. There're domestic records of all sorts, a French public archive would love to have them I imagine. So," she ran down, "that's it, at the moment."

"Tell you what," he said abruptly. "Just inform the heirs that we're leaving the library contents for their disposal, and you, young lady—you pack and come home, quickly."

"Oh no," she protested tiredly. "There's still an enormous litter of stuff, it must be gone through. I've at least two or three more days' work on it, actually it's—" On a sudden and quite unexpectedly to herself, she had broken off.

"What is it?" he demanded. "What's the matter?"

"Nothing really." She had gone dull again. "It's just that I've realised, only this moment, that the house records were all tied up in bundles, but this other stuff—"

"What? what about it?"

"It's all over the floor, churned up anyhow. As if," she conjectured, "someone'd been looking for something in it." Her voice sharpened a little. "I don't know why it didn't occur to me, before."

"Well, well." His voice dismissed it. "The old lady might have messed it up a bit, the deceased—I understand she was peculiar, to say the least."

"I shouldn't wonder," she mumbled, listening again to her own silent voice, *What's it matter, what does anything matter*, meanwhile replying to his injunctions not to overdo, to take care of herself, hurry home . . .

She replaced the receiver, turned, and only then became aware of the auditor—to her end of the conversation, at least.

"Good day, madame," he murmured, bowing, and none too amiably she replied, "You move very quietly, don't you?"

"I am sorry, I—I move like always, I do not wish to disturb you."

She said nothing, her enormous weariness quenching her exasperation; turning to go, she found herself pursued by his voice. "I regret to have gone away, I regret very much, madame." He was anxious and fluent. "It is my illness that comes on so quick, I have not time to tell you, I must see my doctor in Paris at once or else it becomes serious, very serious." He invested a half-smile. "I am sorry if I have discommoded you, madame, but now I am much better, I am ready to work for you again."

Completely disarmed by this for an instant, in another instant she thought coldly, *He's lying*, and found this conclusion running out, again, into overwhelming indifference.

"I see," she answered after the imperceptible pause. "I hope you're better?"

"Oh yes, all better, and now," he pronounced with enthusiasm, "now I shall work for you again."

You will, will you? she thought with a flicker of irony, while replying, "Well, later perhaps."

"But not later, madame, I am all well, I work for you!" There was no let-down in his vim. "Maintenant, maintenant!"

"I'll tell you later." She continued turning away. "If there's anything to do."

"But the heavy things, the books, I carry—"

Mere surprise at such insistence turned her around again to look at him. "I'll tell you," she repeated over-distinctly, "if there's anything to do later on."

Walking off, she heard a last, "But madame!" and continued walking, her thoughts reverting painfully to the scene she had made last night, the disgusting humiliating scene . . . Arriving at the double door of the library she took out its beautiful but massive key that weighed a ton; her first demand on any job was the means of locking up securely. Just inserting the key, the slightest sound made her turn around with a start; the fact that he had succeeded in following her entirely without her knowledge meant that he had taken pains to do so, for the uncarpeted areas of these ancient floors did not lend themselves to such noiselessness . . .

"Madame," he was saying. "It is not kind of you, not fair, I was ill, how could I help being ill—"

"Now see here," she interrupted, her voice dangerously level. "You will go away at once, and stay away. And as for my saying that I would call you in case of need—"

She had not intended any of this; it was her personal misery, the spur to retaliate upon someone, anyone, that kept forcing the words out of her.

"—I shan't," she concluded. "So don't trouble to remain here on my account."

The following silence, stony, seemed to change them both to stone; they stared at each other, motionless, she with sudden colour in her cheeks, he with features gone utterly blank. *You old filth*, he rehearsed silently, *your husband is sleeping with me, me, he will not give it to you, you want it but fat chance, fat chance . . .*

About to open his lips and deliver these sentiments, all at once he checked—not from any definable caution but from something deeper. Fear of Dominic's anger? Or whether fear or not it was somehow *important*, he must think about it . . .

She had turned her back on him and unlocked the door, passed through, and shut it with an undisguised bang. The sound of the key turning again on the other side brought an evil silent amusement to his face as he thought of the servants' back stair, which had probably never occurred to her . . . A jubilation took him, senseless; the conviction that among the papers in the closet, he would know the ones he had buried. Yes, he *would* know it again, he would . . . get in there late at night and look till he found it . . .

She sat at the table methodically separating, sorting and reading another armful of papers from the closet, and all the while still upset over the recent episode. *That creature*, she thought, *nasty little* . . . then forgot it for the real trouble that had kept her awake most of the night, that had haunted her as she sat opposite her husband at breakfast, wordless. The vile scene she had made, screaming and threatening, how did one survive such shame . . .

"What'll I do," she said aloud; her voice had made her start while a sickness rose up in her. *What'll I do, what'll I do*, she repeated to herself, silently—then broke off, indistinctly aware that she had laid aside a paper without even seeing what was on it.

"My God," she muttered, and snatched it back. This was the researcher's bane; one single abstracted moment for whatever cause and you might lose essential references, allusions of the most important . . .

The paper, actually, was not from a coachmaker or similar; her first glance spotted it as a personal communication, and her second as the earliest thing of the sort she had seen so far, 1557. Grateful to whoever had troubled to date his or her letters, she turned it over and saw the signature; the ambassador undoubtedly, the family great man whom her previous research—very sketchy, it was true—had seemed to indicate as a respectable nullity. Still, faintly interested in this first glimpse of him as a person, she began to read the very clear handwriting with comparatively few older forms such as *estes* for *êtes* or *vostre* for *vôtre*; English writing of the same period was usually a nightmare.

Sieur mon père, madame ma mère; je vous me recommende avec tout dévouement et soumission.

Her faint smile acknowledged the resemblance between this, and the contemporary style of English letters to parents: *I recommend myself to you with humble duty and obedience*, and lingered as she continued reading.

In this place are very poor inns and strange architecture. The burghers are rich but heavy and stupid and the native tongue is barbarous. The court is not magnificent. We were received with much politeness. I made my bow to His Royal Highness the Archduke who deigned to speak a few words to me in Latin. He knew of you, my father, and charged me to convey to you and to madame my mother his remembrance and compliments. Forgive me if for lack of time I must cease, I have many documents to prepare for dispatch. Pray do not fear if my letters are infrequent. In this charming land of l'Obéissance des Archiducs, the snows are lying deep and the roads are vile. Monsieur et madame, avec tout devoir et hommages, vostre fils tout dévoué,

Armand Félicien St Luc de Léovil

Now her smile was genuine; in the dullest letter of any period one might stumble on delightful bits.

Where do you live, my pretty maid?

In the Archduke's Obedience, sir, she said.

Only, where was this country? After a moment she half-remembered that it might have been Flanders and Brabant, later called the Spanish and then the Austrian Netherlands, or was she wrong . . . ? But get on with it, get on, she had no time to waste . . .

"What did you do in Paris?" Dominic's casual tone belied his torment of suspicion. "That extra day or so?"

"That was not my fault, the extra day," said Maury with similar casualness. "There was a delay at my bank, they said I came a day too early or some such bêtise, I must come next day. So I was compelled, I must wait."

With whom did you stay overnight? rose as far as the other's lips and no further; with an effort he enquired, "And did you get your money?"

"A little, mon dieu how little!" This at least was true of Cecil's parting present; tranquilly he changed the subject. "That bitch of yours will no longer let me help her."

Dominic, still on the rack of jealousy, took a moment to come to. "What? what was that?"

"The cow, your wife," said the boy with soft cruel distinctness. "She no longer allows me to help. She is angry," he added unnecessarily, "because I went without telling her."

A moment stretched out, wordless. Both men lay still, the elder now fully awakened and plunged in thought, the younger equally deep in what, with him, passed for thought. *You have no money,* silently he rehearsed his growing conviction. *What you gave me for Paris, you had to get it from the woman.* Into his second conviction that he had somehow been swindled crept a thread of caution. *Still, wait till I find out for sure. Or even so, go with you to England? where I may find someone rich, rich . . . ?*

Aloud he said, carelessly, "Vous devez au garage, encore."

"Owe the garage?" Dominic stared. "What for?"

"Oh, a little scratch on the car maybe, not my fault—"

"Hell!"

"—it was not my fault," the boy persisted tranquilly. "I do not even know how it happened."

"All right, all right." His irritation almost escaped in the comment, *I don't wonder that she booted you out,* but aware of the probable reaction, he suppressed it. "Now about the situation with my wife, I'll tell you. Keep out of her way, for the present. Keep out of sight," he repeated emphatically. "For the next three or four days, it can't be any longer than that. By then we'll be going, and I will make arrangements."

The faun merely looked at him, with bright innocent enquiry.

"I'll give you money to travel on." Dominic had heard him plainly. "And I'll meet you in London, by then I'll know just how . . . just where . . ." His voice, in spite of him, betrayed the incertitude of his plans. ". . . don't worry, all will be arranged. You must leave here *after* we go, that's all. You—

you—" Jocular, he had to nerve himself. "You *are* coming with me, aren't you?"

The faun nodded and smiled, thinking meanwhile, *Get in the library, see those papers.*

"You mean it?" Dominic asked fiercely. "You mean it?"

"I say it truly." Already he was walking along the servants' passageway, whose doors had no keys; he had seen to that. *She is not there all day,* he told himself with perfect correctness. *And never late at night, the cow.*

No more of it, she decided; no more sitting opposite him at meals, both of them perfectly silent; it was barbarous, they must manage to speak to each other. If it were he that began she would respond . . . all the while knowing, somehow, that *he* would not begin, that she must take the initiative. *All right,* she answered this inner bidding, *I will, I'll begin.* But not as she had done last night in that tone of tentative gaiety, that timid beckoning of affection . . . she cringed at the remembrance, then thought with renewed determination, *All the same I'll talk to him this time, I won't be uncivilised . . .*

Somehow quieter in her mind she returned to the sight of her desk pleasantly bare and the results of her work so far, all neatly labelled and stacked on two shelves nearby. Getting to her feet with the slowness of extreme fatigue, she went to the closet for a look at the documents still scattered on the floor. Not a great deal left; at this rate two days, three at most, should polish off the lot. Yawning now, rolling her head to relieve the pain in her back, straightening violently for the benefit of her stinging shoulder-blades, she locked the door as usual behind her before trudging upstairs for a lie-down before dinner.

"I'm very nearly through in there." She had begun without

preamble, rushing it very likely, but anything more accomplished was beyond her. "With the stuff in the closet."

"Oh?" He responded at once and pleasantly, impelled—as she knew—by the same dread of continuing silence as herself. "And is it still all business stuff, or—"

"Letters, now." The plunge taken, she went on resolutely. "I've got down to letters, quite a cache of them."

"Interesting? anything valuable?"

"Not valuable, but interesting in a way." Her own antiquarian passion gave her voice an unconscious lift. "From the man who's going to be ambassador, Armand de Léovil. He's not ambassador yet, though, I haven't got that far."

"I see."

"He begins in 1557 as a young secretary." Well, at the worst he was pretending interest; his tone was an invitation to go on. "In a sort of trade commission to the Low Countries, and he writes to his parents. Then the years go by, he's writing from Spain and Austria and all over. By 1570 he's married, he writes mostly to his wife. Then in 1580 or so, he's become Count."

"Yes?" He still seemed moderately receptive. "And also ambassador?"

"Not ambassador yet, not for a long time. That's what . . . what's wrong with him, come to think." She rallied herself to explain. "He's a disappointed man, disappointed in his career, at least that's my impression. He's on ambassadorial staffs but never top dog—you can feel it more and more in his letters."

"Can you? how?"

"Oh, they've become . . . peevish, bad-tempered. His earlier letters are quite nice and affectionate, but by 1580 that's all over." On a sudden pang, she smiled faintly. "He only writes to his wife about estate business, very dictatorial and all the time finding fault. He's still away a lot, of course." All at once, seeing how much his interest had been forced from the way it declined, a deathly tiredness overwhelmed her; she fought it enough to add, "Of course when he becomes ambassador to Elizabeth, he may be interesting again."

"Yes, he may." His tone was now perfunctory. "Let's hope it'll give the old boy a lift."

"Oh, by the way." A sort of panic forced it out; he was receding from her, she would not let that fatal wordlessness clamp down on them again, she would *not*. "That creature that walked out on me, that Maurice or whatever his name is—"

"Mm?" he asked with masterly uninterest.

"Will you believe he had the nerve to appear again out of nowhere and tell me he was all ready to go to work again? And smiling that *smile* of his." She snorted with disgust. "Kind of him, wasn't it?"

With every nerve alert and with the nuance of boredom he returned, "You sent him packing, I take it?"

"You take it correctly."

"Actually it seems to me—" perfectly contrary to his first intention, he came out with the lie "—it seems to me I saw him leaving, at least he was carrying a case of some sort. All his earthly, I shouldn't wonder."

"I hope so." She was subsiding. "If ever I see him hereabouts again I'll ring the solicitor. He'll be in real trouble, I can promise him that."

"I shouldn't think he'd return." Dismissive, he indicated the tray just brought in. "Shall we have coffee here, or—?"

"Here," she said too quickly. The painful remembrance of last night combined with the painful knowledge that, for all her effort, she had done no more than bore him. "Here's all right."

IX

Maury, fully dressed for once, lay on his bed in the small shabby room that his constant neglect contrived to make disreputable. It was about eleven in the morning, the day outside palely bright. His gaze was distant, his stillness entire and profound, a gift he shared with animals lying in wait; the infrequent motion of his eyelids and the nearly imperceptible rhythm of his breathing the only variation in his movelessness. Such mind as he possessed had now discarded his Parisian resentments and fixed itself, malignly, on the one who had most recently given him offence. As his thoughts wove themselves about her his jaw began to move forward and back in a soundless gritting of teeth. That *espèce d'ordure*, that *chiot*. . . . .

And additional darkness seemed to settle on him as he began reviewing his last night's exploit, his secret invasion of the library via the servants' passage, which she had not troubled or not been able to shut off. It had been well past midnight yet he dared not turn on the chandelier; that blazing light might be visible under the door, or past the drawn window-curtains if anyone happened to look out of the window . . .

With his electric torch he had shuffled over the papers still on the closet floor, a good many, picking up and dropping

143

them at random; finding that so far as the thing went that he was searching for he had lost all idea of its appearance, in fact had he really ever looked at it? quite probably not . . . It was the torch that warned him, dulling and blinking in signal of expiration; he never renewed the batteries till they failed. Consigning his quest to hell he retreated from the closet; the torch's last dying glimmer showed him the results of the hag's work, orderly piles of documents filling two nearby shelves. For a moment he played with the idea of throwing them on the floor and pissing on them, then with a half-sigh gave it up. Such an indulgence would betray his presence, and for the moment—only for the moment—he would obey the old boy's injunction to keep out of sight.

From these abortive episodes his mind returned, with all the more savagery, to the person responsible; she continued before his eyes during a last despairing résumé of his position. This rotten thing he had hidden was a lost cause, musty stink and all. No one would help him dispose of it, no one. In this bleakness one gleam of comfort shone out, one only. The manuscript or whatever one called it would be, in the end, *her* affair, this expert of the books; anything that might come of it, credit or money, would be hers alone. Yes, but there was a way of preventing that, an easy way . . .

The change that came over his face, the smiling stony evil, seemed actually to increase rather than lessen his beauty. Rising briskly he rooted out the magazine that held the manuscript, took a few old newspapers from an unlimited assortment, made sure he had matches on him, and left the room. Stealthily he moved down to the second floor, turned right toward the extreme end, and entered the last door. As he expected, it was a bedroom; of such lower class that he peered anxiously to see if there were a fireplace . . . yes, very small, but a small one would do. Just beginning to rip the newspaper into sheets, he paused an instant. Had there been some-

thing about the fireplaces, they were not to be used . . . ?
"Ah, *merde*," he shrugged, speaking aloud, and resumed tearing and shredding the stuff he had brought until, lighting it, he had a quick bright funeral pyre. Then pulling the heap of old pages from the magazine he began gouging it up by handfuls and throwing them into the flames. Actually the thing seemed to help in its own extermination, crumbling and breaking rather than tearing, depositing a dry shower of bits before the agency of its immolation.

As a small return for all her slogging the contents of the closet seemed to gain in interest, even if not importantly. Almost all the letters, with a few trifling exceptions, were now from the future ambassador Armand, who became—so far as she could see—more peevish and cantankerous from day to day. His wife, poor woman, got the whole brunt of it; beside criticising and scolding her for unsatisfactory reports on their estate, he burdened her with numerous sour reproofs for their children, to whom (apparently) he never wrote directly. Keeping track of these children's names she counted up to five, which might not be all of them by a long shot. "Poor thing," she murmured aloud to the wife, while disengaging the next leaf and seeing—almost at first glance—that at last he had come into his reward; at long last he was full ambassador, and to England; the date was 1596. With unconscious anticipation she bent to the creased and dusty papers, the faded ink; this was the last chance for something remarkable or arresting to turn up . . . and at last, clearly, she had entered a new and even moderately fascinating territory.

First of all it was evident that the sour and disappointed Armand had come at once under the spell of Elizabeth, only his manner of doing so was deliciously funny. As a Frenchman it was a point of honour to denigrate her; actually in the same breath he liked and disliked, admired and despised, and approved and disapproved of her, without mercy. Even now, an old woman, she seemed constantly to mystify and even upset him: *She is an evil old being who appears in a different wig each day, some say she is bald as an egg. In my position I cannot enquire of her ladies who are as old and ugly as herself. Her figure is still beautiful and slender and she carries herself like a queen. She first spoke Latin to me, admirably, then changed to excellent French. She has lost so many teeth that she is often indistinct, yet in anger her voice becomes clearer, at least those who hear her cannot pretend to misunderstand her. She likes to be surrounded by young and handsome men, these miserable creatures play the ardent suitor and pretend to adore her. All of them are in secret communication with her great-nephew James of Scotland, a possible heir, and secretly receive money from him . . .*

"Well!" she exclaimed aloud, then sat back to revise her report to Uncle Frederick and to wonder—in view of her personal misery—at her own power of pleasure and excitement. There was no doubt that this section of the letters would invite spirited bidding at auction, especially by American universities and collectors. On the other hand, it might become increasingly evident that the French authorities would forbid taking them out of France . . . Her mind played with this daunting possibility before, dismissing it, she bent hungrily to the next missives.

She understands business very well, and when she does not it is my impression that she pretends, at doing which she is a past mistress. She is after all a very secret sort of being and a great liar at need, perhaps no more so than any other ruler.

"Ah, now you're making excuses for her," she murmured aloud, thinking at the same time that no other ruler, in Armand's whole diplomatic life, had ever evoked such streams of eloquence from him; it was as if—literally—he could not stop talking about her.

*They say she played the virginals admirably at one time,
but no more. At least they do not try to tell me she sang, with
that crow's voice of hers. There is talk that she has had a
child by Lessitère whom she loved, her breasts do not support
this story but one never knows. She is wonderfully courteous
and agreeable to me, this is because there are presently no dis-
sensions between us. If such arose, I would not trust to her
continued affability. But her manner, when in procession she
shows herself to the mob, I have never seen surpassed for a
graciousness easy and truly royal.*

"You're practically in love with the old girl, Armand," she
muttered aloud. "You made a good stab at Leicester, too,"
and actually laughed—before becoming aware, all at once,
that her task was over; beside some scraps, a single letter
remained. Somehow badly jolted, she sat a moment in total
blankness. This was it then; this was all of it. Nothing to do
now but ring London again, tell Palgrave of this unexpected
development, consult with him about the necessity of notify-
ing not only the heirs but also the national documentary
archives, investigate the possibility of getting permission to
export this correspondence . . .

With her mind on this, distractingly, she had reached for
the remaining letter before she woke to its condition: most of
a page but in worse condition than any so far, also of a fragil-
ity that made any handling inadvisable. Changing tactics, she
teased it before her with cautious movements of two fingers,
straightened it in the same manner, and bent to read. The sal-
utation was missing, also part of the opening and closing sen-
tences.

*. . . in this uncouth language which I still understand
badly and have no desire to understand better. I was obliged
to sit for two hours while it went on and on, all of them
laughing madly and myself dying of ennui and a desire to
sleep. At the end of it she summoned the lot of them before*

her and they obeyed, still dressed in their foolish dress, bowing and grinning and smelling of sweat and paint. Imagine to yourself if you can our King, our Henri, thus degrading his royalty. I tell you the woman grows stranger as she grows old and sometimes conducts herself like a fool. Do not repeat this to anyone, it is my command. She singled out one of these buffons, an older man, and spoke with him an unsuitable length of time. Then she said something which I missed, and another buffon brought forward, with profound obeisances, a dirty heap of papers sewn up with cord. Now to my horror she turns herself and offers me this nasty thing, saying in English, My Lord Ambassador, keep this copy in remembrance of the first English play you have seen and which . . .

The shock in her brain at the next words—the sort of stroke —paralysed not only her power of thought, her power of movement, but seemed to suspend life itself; in this waking daze she sat stupid and inert, all but the savage thumping of her heart against her side. "It's not true," she heard a dull voice mutter after an interval, "it's not true." After another while she stirred experimentally, which produced a pain that lanced through her neck and arms; she tried again and was able to move, but weakly, weakly . . .

Still half stupefied, with cataleptic slowness she slid a sheet of fresh heavy paper under the letter and enclosed the whole in a notebook. Then she had to apply herself to the problem of rising, getting a grip on the notebook, tottering to the door . . . as she unlocked it a spasm of weakness pushed her against the lintel; suppose she fainted, dropped what she was carrying, suppose the old brittle paper broke to bits in the fall . . .

The lethal strengthlessness passed, leaving no worse behind than a faint sickness and a trembling in her legs. *Your bad luck,* she told them without mercy as they got her up two long flights of stairs to the attic where Dominic worked.

His back was turned to her as she opened the door; he was holding two pieces together while Alex worked on them, both men totally absorbed. Alex saw her first, and the sight was enough to strike his hand motionless as he stared, then said uncertainly, "Miss . . . ?" Dominic, at the word, turned about; he also was startled, pausing first then rising hastily and saying, "Val? is something the matter—?"

"No, no," she managed, "I'm all right, I'm perfectly . . ." then controlled her failing voice and said, "I must speak to you." She sounded weak, abrupt, and so commanding that no question was possible, let alone refusal. While surprise still immobilised him she had turned and walked out of the door; after a moment he followed. Before he could make a sound she commanded again, "Not here," and started downstairs. She was ready to fall to the bottom, he could tell by her clutch on the railing, and got a little ahead of her in case. Not even noticing this apparently, once they were on the level she moved ahead of him, opened a bedroom door and walked in. Here she delicately opened a notebook she was carrying, as delicately placed it on a table, and said, "Read that." She motioned feebly. "Don't touch, just read it," then fell perfectly quiet. After a single uncomprehending glance he bent over it; with her eyes glued to his face, she was well prepared for the gasp that came out of him and could still see—as in letters of fire—what had caused it.

—*the first English play you have seen and which was written by Guillaume—the other name I did not catch, a barbarous sound like Schak-pire or similar. The worse for me you will say, and you are right.*

The pun, she had thought limply, untranslatable.

Since she held this object out to me I was obliged to take it and bow. One of these clowns, the scribbler of this nonsense I suppose, was also bowing; if he had come an inch nearer me, I swear I would have spurned him with my foot. The Queen

saw my distaste and smiled with malice so as to display her
three or four black teeth remaining in front. When I returned
home however I did not at once cast her gift into the rubbish.
Our Maître des Divertissements at Court is always seeking
novelties, he might adapt this nonsense to amuse His Maj-
esty. I send it to you therefore, if I wait until my demission it
may be thrown away or otherwise lost. Keep it safely till my
return, even so small a thing may be a means to favour. His
Majesty takes pleasure in laughing and surely these English
laughed. Also he is much disposed to discourses on love, and
the title of this idiocy seems to be Travail d'Amour Gagné or
some such . . .

Into the following silence—long? short?—she mumbled,
"This is the . . . the second allusion that . . . that such a
play ever existed . . ."

"What? What's that?"

"There's one . . . only one single mention, contemporary
. . . that there was such a play as *Love's Labour's Won*. This
is the . . ."

He made a sound, inarticulate.

". . . the second one, the second . . . proof," she finished
almost inaudibly.

"Well," he began, had trouble with his voice, and tried
again. "It only remains to see whether it's . . . it's still . . ."

"Wait," she broke in, her own voice sharpening. "Maybe
I've something here, maybe I . . ."

With deathly care she removed the precious fragment from
the notebook, then turned the pages shakily and roughly. "I
made some notes on the family, before I came . . ." She
began reading half aloud. ". . . Austria . . . Low Countries
. . . yes! Here it is." She raised her voice. "Ambassador to
England 1596–1600. Died . . ." She had to swallow. "Died
1600." She transferred her gaze to Dominic, listening in car-

ven silence. "It sounds as if he were ill when he got home, and died almost at once. So perhaps he never—" she drew a loud shaken breath "—never did have time to hand it over as he planned, it may . . . it m-may . . ."

"—still be in the house." He straightened from the table on which he was leaning and drew a loud breath on his own account. "Yes."

"But you—you've already searched the whole place over, haven't you—"

"I've searched in a way, tested every desk and cabinet for secret drawers, that sort of thing." He took another breath. "But I didn't look for hiding-places in the house itself, in the *structure* of the—"

"Oh, Dominic." In her state of unrecovered shock, she still wanted to laugh. "Why would they hide it? You're talking as if those people of centuries ago took our view of it. To them it would be nothing but a piece of rubbish."

"You're right, I'm a fool. All the same—" his voice revived "—supposing some later person hid it—"

"If a later person had found it," she brushed this aside, "the whole world would have known of it years ago."

"All the same," he said harshly, "we'll start taking the place apart, now."

"Do you remember," she asked dreamily, "those sixteenth-century women who lined pie-plates with illuminated manuscripts from the monasteries? And this thing wasn't ornamental, just a dirty old prompt copy."

"And do *you* remember," he retorted, "the Boswell papers, stuffed in an old box and left in an outbuilding for a couple of hundred years?"

"Oh yes, yes, we must hunt.—Dominic." Her voice broke a little. "If we find it . . . what do you suppose will happen?"

"We'll have to report it," he said after a moment. "To the

French authorities. We risk a hideous scandal if we try to sneak it out."

"And after you've reported it," she murmured. "Then what?"

"Then the French government will impound it."

Of course, she contributed silently.

"And after that they'll set up a committee to examine it, Shakespearean scholars—" He broke off. "What are you laughing at?"

"The committee." She burbled weakly. "When they come to choose it—the bloodshed."

"I daresay." His token smile vanished. "It'll all be in French hands—publication, production rights, everything. They'll hand most of what they get to the family, and end by putting the thing on exhibit. With armed guards day and night," he concluded. "In the Louvre, most likely."

"Shakespeare," she murmured half-wittedly, "wouldn't care for that."

"Neither will the English public," he retorted. "Come on, let's get cracking."

"And *this*—" she indicated the precious letter "—what'll we do about it?"

"We'll keep our mouths shut," he said decisively. "Easy to say it was in unexamined papers sent to England."

"Oh yes, yes." She hesitated. "The letter alone—what do you think it'll make?"

"Unpredictable, absolutely unpredictable. But one thing I'll tell you." He spoke with disgust and certainty. "The Americans'll get it."

Even the ground floor was included in the exploration—to the silent incredulity and sense of uselessness that she knew better than to express, leavened by the thought: well, an old chest of papers or similar *might* have been stowed away down here at one time or another, it might have . . . no old chest or anything like it appeared in the vast old kitchen with its mammoth fireplaces or in the warren of store-rooms long given over to the spider, dust and dirt and unidentifiable trash of every kind. At one time she interrupted their progress to halt, stand still, and declare, "I smell smoke."

"Smoke?" He stood for a moment, questing the air. "From the cooker I daresay. Come on!" and actually—when for the sake of thoroughness they invaded the small kitchen in use—their perfunctory search was accompanied by Clémence's grumblings about the cooker which was smoking a little, visibly.

"I said it was the cooker," Dominic reminded her on their way upstairs.

She said nothing, aware of the lingering smart in her nostrils, assuredly fainter, and trailed him silently as he went through rooms, side-passages and cubicles, omitting none; she had to acknowledge more and more his power of observation and his thoroughness. Also he had been concentrating on the possibility of secret hiding-places; when nothing materialised she admitted, always silently, that he had been quite right to look for them.

Not until he was almost through on the second floor did an intention of her own come to life, belatedly; she began opening the obscurer doors at random, murmuring to herself, "Where is it, where . . ." She opened another. "Ah! here." It was a narrow wooden flight unknown to her and intimately familiar to him; absorbed in her search she had missed his sudden stopping, his involuntary start and alarmed aspect. As he stood wordless, completely unprepared for this development, she started to mount, then turned. "Aren't you coming?"

"Up there?" His heart had started beating hard, his mind whirled crazily; Maury, Maury . . . the lazy little fool might still be in bed, he had an endless capacity for lying about. If he were there she was sure to find him and what the outcome might be there was no telling. His lie leaped to his mind, his own lie of having seen him depart . . . to say nothing of his pretence, constant from the beginning, of not knowing the boy at all, of having had nothing to do with him . . .

"There?" he repeated. "What for?"

"Just to make a thorough job of it."

"I've seen that part," he shrugged. "It's nothing but old empty holes, servants' bedrooms—"

"Dominic! the smoke, it's coming from up here—" She started pelting upward. "We've got to see—"

He was on her heels at once, no less alarmed, and for double reasons. The smell, as she said, was suddenly powerful and acrid; they must find where it was coming from, no two ways about it . . .

A greyness was veiling the air as she neared the top of the stairs; just as she climbed through the opening to the attic floor, she received a double shock. To steady herself she had rested her right hand on the wall a moment, and snatched it away; the wall was hot. Before she could make a sound of warning a heavy cloud of smoke came puffing out through the (apparently) solid wall, and immediately after this she saw, through a black fog, a naked figure emerge from somewhere. It was running, trying to put on some sort of garment while running, it came toward them running. And all this in silence, utter silence . . .

Broken by a confusion of slight sounds either simultaneous or rapidly succeeding each other in this landscape of imminence. First was the rapid thud of bare feet, then a sort of soft refined belch as a tongue of fire wafted through the wall and gently licked at the body running past, withdrawing at once as if in apology; transfixed with unexpectedness she saw one side of this body gleaming beautiful, intact, the other side lightly veiled for the fraction of a moment by the negligent touch of flame . . .

The third sound in this soundless landscape was voices: the naked man's cry of angry pain together with Dominic's shout of "Maury! Maury!" as he pushed her aside, blindly, and darted forward. He was supporting the graceful form in spite of its evident wish not to be supported, its furious but feeble attempts to wrest itself free. To his wife, as she stood paralysed, he gasped, "Ring the firehouse, quick."

Still in her shock—of revelation it was true, yet still deeper in some secondary shock, plunged in it all at once—she took a witless step forward.

"I'll manage, I'll manage—ring them!" he yelled savagely. "Move! *move!*"

X

For over twenty-four hours now she had fought and fought to lay her hand on the key or memory, whatever it was, that would unlock the trance in which she was imprisoned. At this moment of late afternoon she was lying on her bed as it chanced, but in bed or out she was in the merciless grip of the thing, the same thing that had laid its clutch on her yesterday . . . only, what was it? One single certainty she did have so far as it went, one absolute conviction: that her state of struggling in a vacuum for something unknown had begun at the moment—the precise moment—when the flame had waved so sleepily out of the wall and Dominic had sprung toward the boy with a cry of anguish . . . yes, it had happened to her in that moment.

Also in that same moment of shattering comprehension, it was true, she had seen the end of her marriage. But even this, even this cataclysm of awakening, was a minor consideration compared with the other thing that had fastened its paralytic grip on her, not loosening for one single moment since yesterday, not once, not once . . . from mere exhaustion of battering at something that would not come, she thought again of her present state of mind. No grief, no regret, that was the astonishing thing; she was free, free of her burden of love, the heavy humiliating weight of unwanted love. A marvelous thing, release, she ought to be on her knees thanking God or whoever was responsible . . . and yet again she knew that even this release was not the important thing, it was secondary to what she was trying to bring back; the other thing, *other*. . . .

At that point came the knock at her door. Still nailed motionless in her waking dream she hardly noticed; after moments the knock was repeated. Half scrambling and half falling out of bed as she went to answer, she thought maliciously, *Well, it's taken you twenty-four hours to pluck up courage to speak to me* . . .

"Val," he said in a low voice at once peremptory and uncertain. "Can I talk to you?"

"Of course," she said in an expressionless voice.

He made as if to come in; at once, not giving way, she said, "Not here," and came out, closing the door behind her. "We can go downstairs, if you like."

He nodded silently. Through the heavy post-fire stench they started descending, she walking ahead steadily and yet with a growing restiveness that—to her own astonishment— she perceived belatedly to be anger. She had been about to discover or define something in relation to her puzzle if he had not intruded then, *then*, with his knocking. Why could he not have come ten minutes later, even five, instead of when he had . . . They had reached a room, the same room where she had offered herself and been rejected. She did not even notice; in her present state all lesser things had somehow disappeared. She sat down in the same chair as then, he likewise in the chair he had occupied. As he seemed to have difficulty in starting she asked, "How is he?"

"Not bad." He laughed constrainedly. "Foul tempered— very sorry for himself."

During another pause she realised for the first time that he had not tried to establish the boy in his bedroom next to hers, he had had the decency to put him somewhere farther off . . . Remembering his melodramatic support of the angry boy who did not wish to be supported, she did not allow her ghost of a smile to reach her face. Instead she enquired, with composure, "Has a doctor seen him?"

"I wanted to call one." He shrugged. "But he took it so outrageously I had to give in. It's not a burn," he explained. "Just a very light . . . scorching you might say, on one side— and so superficial that it'll clear itself up in a few days, most likely. He's young, you know, in excellent health . . ."

"I see," she murmured as his voice ran down.

"Actually," he offered an awkward postscript, "he has no pain at all. I got butter in the village, pounds of it, and he spreads it all over himself. A bit messy, but it takes care of the pain entirely."

There followed a silence long or short, indistinguishable; half an eternity, considering the recollections packed into it. Discovery of fire; the accompanying terror and helplessness, arrival of the firemen, efficient for all their violent and dramatic shouting; everyone in the house herded onto the lawn, the boy carried out wrapped in blankets and solicitously laid on a bench. Carefully refraining from looking at him, all the same she had been aware of his frantic peevishness which Dominic tried constantly and unsuccessfully to soothe. Then meanwhile, along with the whole population of the village, the arrival of the sisters; brought like the rest of the scavengers by the promise of calamity, only theirs was also the promise of loss; their outcry, Dominic torn between caring for his invalid and assuring them that the fire was nowhere near the treasure in the attic, there was no danger of that.

Finally, the fire-chief—when the blaze was extinguished— insisting on the presence of the sisters to inspect the scene of the fire, in some remote upstairs part of the chateau. Dominic had gone along; she felt herself uninvited so remained where she was, as far as possible from Maury. Curiously enough she had not yet begun thinking, not consciously. While this fog still wrapped her the inspecting party had returned, and the fire-chief with them; now he was explaining to Clémence that in this case smoke must have backfired from the obstructed chimney, her *poêle* would be all right now, as good as new, don't worry . . .

She half-returned to the present moment and the half-realisation of Dominic still there, sitting opposite her . . . only now, out of nowhere, conviction dealt her a blow as with a club: that he was somehow involved in the distant happening she had been trying to force into existence. At once her common-sense sprang forcibly to reject this theory. The unknown event had been far away, that much she knew, it had been long before she had met him or known of his existence. Yet once more he was *there*, he was in it somehow . . . she gave up, exhausted, coming back all the way to now. Also to his voice, speaking to her . . .

"Val."

"Oh! sorry, sorry . . ." as if summoned from a great distance she spoke too quickly and loudly, and then—with a desire of evasion or putting-off too vague for definition—asked, "Did the fire do much damage?"

"No." He said it after a moment, obviously side-tracked. "One chimney burnt-out at the very end of the house, one fireplace in a second-floor room full of muck, and the room it's in soaking wet, of course." He was plainly uninterested in going on, yet was constrained to add, "The fire-chief said the chimney at that end's done for too—there's a crack in it clear from the attic floor down to the second."

Silent, with eyes far away and mouth half-open, she saw the

pale yellow flame reach out and negligently eclipse, no, half-eclipse, the beautiful body.

"Thank God," a voice was saying remotely, "it's at the opposite end of the house from where the furniture is."

Had she answered or not answered, did it make any difference one way or the other . . .

"Val." By the change in his tone he was returning to what she had interrupted; he bent forward, at the same time giving an impression of squaring himself. "You saw . . . you saw how it is with . . . with me and Maury . . . ?"

"I'm sorry for the other evening," she blurted without will or intention. "I'll give you a divorce."

Startled and brought up short—a fact which escaped her—he had to take a moment to re-compose himself and start again. "But see here, we're civilised, we can talk this over—" He had given the utmost thought to his conduct of this interview, yet now in the moment itself cursed his utterance, broken, hurried and uneasy. "Look, Val, I've always been that way, I don't apologise, it's something one can't help. Very good, you'll say I—I shouldn't have married, and you'll be perfectly right. The fact is . . ." He paused, again gathering himself visibly. ". . . the truth is, if I'd sized you up as a passionate woman, I'd never have considered marriage. Never, not in a thousand years." He breathed in, harshly. "Aside from being sorry about this—tremendously sorry—I was right about that one thing. You aren't passionate, you know, there isn't a vestige of passion in you. Is there, now? Be truthful, it's all I ask. But I *am* right, aren't I? I'm right?"

During the long pause that he gave her to consider her answer, she was—instead—engrossed in something totally different. Who was it sitting there and putting urgent questions to her, which as a matter of fact she had only half-heard? Her husband, the man she had been in love with so totally, so submissively? There he sat in all the pride of his handsomeness, spiritedness, intelligence, all the qualities that had overthrown her, yet all in a moment they were not there, they had not only ceased to attract but even faintly displeased her. Yet it was the same man, the same body, or was it not the same . . . Without time even to consider the thunderbolt that can destroy love, let alone define or name it, she tried to pin this element of growing repulsion. His mouth? No, his mouth was the same, a finely-moulded line. Or again was something wrong with it, she could not decide, she was in no state to decide . . . Violently she recalled her attention; he was leaning forward, watching her every expression.

"It's so, isn't it?" he repeated, but gently now, cozeningly. "It's not an extraordinary lack, you know. I'm willing to bet most people have no idea of passion, if it comes to that. It's a gift, special."

Well, perhaps, she said silently and with unexpected promptitude; her mind must have cleared another degree. *But I might have learned to be passionate, I think I could have learned. Yes, I might!* she threw at him loudly and still silently. *If you'd been a man—!* She broke off short, scared at her pitiless words and looking at him with apology, as though she had spoken them.

"You love to be petted and made much of, like a child," he was saying even more gently. "But that's all, isn't it? All there is to it?"

"Very likely," she said, for the sake of saying something. "Yes, I suppose . . ."

"All right." He was leaning forward still more intently with the effect, but not the actuality, of having cut her off. He had not cut her off; she had simply run down. "Now look, dear Val. And don't be suspicious of that *dear,* I'm fond of you, I am. I admire you professionally, I respect you more than I can say. I think you're one of the finest . . . beings . . . I've ever met. I couldn't be talking to you like this, otherwise. I'd never have tried, I shouldn't dream of it."

As he paused again, her gaze had re-clamped itself upon him with more and more intensity, as if seeing him for the first time. Always with a curious wonderment she itemised his other perfections: his tallness, his clear skin slightly tanned, his splendid figure with broad shoulders and trim waist, his hands beautifully shaped yet masculine . . . *Not one bodily thing to betray what he is,* came to her involuntarily, then— on wondering at the coldness with which she had thought it— suddenly knew the answer.

"Look, Val."

Now he was speaking not only softly, but with another quality that all at once roused her anger and resistance. As he continued she realised the cause of her resentment: the new thing in his voice, the *confidence* . . . *You think it's going swimmingly, don't you?* she snarled at him without a sound, then all at once was riven by another flash of prescience. *And I know exactly what you're going to say—!*

"Is there any reason, any good reason," he was pursuing, "why we should break up? Your real passion, I mean your only real passion, is your work. I know that, I've always known it. We . . . we're at one there, we've a thousand things in common in that respect. We could continue as we are now, living in the same house. I promise you—I guarantee you—that the other thing'll be out of sight, so far as you're concerned. You'll never see it, it won't exist. Anyway—" His voice clouded a little; he cleared his throat. "—anyway, most women like to be married, they'd much rather be married than not. Do you think," he argued, with a new onset of vigour, "that ours'll be the only household with such an arrangement? I've known plenty of them, successful ones too, plenty—!"

He broke off, scanning her face with an anxiety which she

suddenly found pleasant; simultaneously she was thinking, *And you're planning to bring this creature to London, of course*, and again with malicious amusement saw the boy fighting off the anxious loving embrace.

"He'll come with me to London, of course," he said like an echo. "And wherever I find him to live, it'll be completely out of your orbit. Completely," he repeated. "I assure you."

Yes, she thought again. Her sudden drop from hatred to a momentary submissiveness surprised her. *Yes, you're in love.*

"Can't help it," he muttered, again as if she had spoken. "Can't help being in love."

"No," she said calmly out of her liberation, always more aware of the incongruous elements that made up this liberation. Shock of discovery was in it, shock of death, the death of love; all that was a great deal to happen to you in one moment . . . *Fool*, she addressed herself, *even the final release can be quicker than that, still quicker*, then all at once was possessed by the other thing, *other*; the same torment, now more restive, that had been growing in her since the moment when her life fell to pieces before her eyes . . .

"What do you say?" his voice recalled her, rousing in her the same irritation at this recall. "Or at least, will you think it over?"

"Think it over?" she repeated vacantly.

"Whether with this new situation," he rehearsed patiently, "you and I can stay together."

Fully awakened she let a pause elapse on purpose, long enough to let him taste the pleasures of suspense; her inward and evil smile never got to the surface. He had put his position baldly, she would put hers with equal baldness.

"No," she said too gently.

For an instant he was taken aback, but recovered. "Val, just take a little time before you decide—"

"I couldn't go along with such an arrangement," she continued softly, and let her smile be seen. "I couldn't possibly."

He seemed to waken suddenly to her gentle amusement, gentle voice, gentle rejection and what underlay all of them; as suddenly he blurted, "I've made a mistake."

"Yes," she replied evenly. "I think you have."

"Oh Christ, what a fool . . ." in spite of his distraction he glanced at his wrist and was shaken. "Hell, I should be up-stairs giving a hand, a lorry's due any moment.—Val, I'm sorry, sorry, got no time now, see you later—" He vanished.

Yes, she thought, echoing his epithet, *you are one, aren't you, a considerable fool,* all the while standing and listening. His departing footsteps were quick and dull on the drawing-room rug, then quick and loud in the marble-paved hall, then differently loud on the wooden staircase . . . . silence.

I was to be the complaisant wife, was I? she spoke to him in the silence. *You have another guess coming. Two guesses, in fact.* Her laugh of amusement was small and ugly. *Did you think you'd keep your job with Palgrave's? You'll see, my lad, you'll see,* then all at once she realised the dimension, the true enormous dimension of her luck. Suppose it had turned out that he loved another women; what a horror it would have been, what an unhealing wound, a death-wound . . .

"I'm lucky," she told herself strangely, half-aloud, then stood vacant again. How still it was, still as death; hard to be-lieve in yesterday's commotion whose souvenirs lingered ac-tively, above all the stink that abraded your nostrils harshly if you breathed in deep, even this far from where the fire had been . . .

Curiosity began touching her, vague at first then stronger. What damage had the blaze done, why not go see, she might as well; her work was over, she had nothing to do but wrestle with some ancient phantom that refused to materialise . . .

She went upstairs to the second floor, turned right into the long corridor of yesterday, and stopped dead. The smell was noticeably more vicious; she followed it and could see, farther ahead, an area blackened and water-soaked and scattered with the smaller detritus of destruction. Venturing farther along she could see the door of the attic peremptorily closed by planks nailed across it and a red sign, *Danger!* Alongside of it was a crack in the wall that fell down from the ceiling, obvious continuation of the crack overhead; the same crack through which had breathed the single yellow flame like some fabled bird's wing. . . .

She went past it and found herself at the end of the corridor; a final door stood closed but little damaged. Without conscious thought she turned the knob and walked into a bedroom small and mean by comparison with the front range of them on the same floor but quite good enough for a lady-in-waiting, say, or a secretary. The room was drenched, no other word for it; furniture and bed giving off the unclean reek of wet wool, a crumpled hillock of rug in one corner still shedding drops, wet paper beginning to loosen from the wet walls, and here the post-fire stench cut like a knife . . . She took a step toward the fireplace and saw that it was horridly choked by a black wet mass, obviously fallen from higher up in the chimney. Here and there about the hearth were strewn various bits and pieces, even shreds of paper with a semi-liquid look . . .

Wondering vaguely why she had troubled to come here, what on earth she could have expected to see, she stood motionless again with bowed head and eyes fixed sightlessly on the carpet . . . becoming slowly aware of something just at her feet, a scrap of paper larger than most; only her automatic professionalism made her bend and pick it up.

The instant she had it in her hand her vacant stillness passed into a petrified stillness. Unbelieving, bewildered, she stared at the fragment with its look of great age, at its few lines of English written in palest ink, its torn and tattered edges that truncated the words all about . . . with foundering wits she fixed herself upon it and with difficulty made out:

> Dec. O leav me praie with this my sorrowe
>   Tis my companion my estate my
>   earthlie dower
> Val. Nay madam nay: greife no dower is
>   But death a lesser death an end
>   before the end
>   Which like th'infective

Her legs gave way under her so suddenly that she staggered, almost fell, and was only saved by chancing to pitch against the damp wall.

The delirium subsided after an unrealised interval; again she began to think, after a fashion. The thing she was holding, the ancient damp survival; on its own the impact would have been powerful enough, but after the ambassador's letter it was shattering. This must be a remnant of Elizabeth's gift or rather her malicious travesty of a gift . . . but all this aside, how did it come to be up here in this impossible place? Why was it not in the library where one would expect it to be? Unless . . .

A gasp tore from her, its violent pain refracting in her throat, chest and head; ignoring it, she pursued her new thought with the fixity of an animal after prey. If that creature, that corrupt boy, had had anything to do with it; if he had found the play in the library and brought it up here to burn . . . an access of cold common sense stopped her together with a sound of self-derision. Feebly holding on to her theory, she crossed swords with the mere improbability of it. He was almost completely illiterate, Dominic's Maury, imagine his being able to isolate this one thing out of family papers containing other ambassadorial relics in Spanish, Italian, even a few in English . . .

She returned to the bit of damp paper. *His* writing? Perhaps not, not for a certainty. With a new play in rehearsal four or five copies would be necessary for director, prompter, devisers of scenes, the author would certainly not do all of them. The scanty survival must be submitted to experts . . . vaguely she remembered that his handwriting had changed very much in his later life . . . All at once she groaned aloud under a ravaging sense of loss, loss. Shakespeare's lost play, Schubert's lost symphonies, paintings and sculptures lost by the thousand in sieges, fires, shipwreck . . . That vile mass in the fireplace: it must be dredged out and examined minutely, however useless it must be done . . . *Tomorrow, tomorrow,* she thought in a panic of weakness, *I'll do it tomorrow.*

Her eyes, coming back again to the precious remnant, were different now with quest, with enquiry. One woman was consoling another, they sounded like women. *Val* for Valeria? Valentine? She preferred Valeria, her own name. "You're right, you know," all at once she addressed her namesake of four centuries ago. "Grief isn't my end, it's not my end at all," then felt how the dampness of the wall was coming through her sleeve, and straightened abruptly. *I've got to lie down,* she excused herself to Valeria, this time in silence, and started moving shakily. Yet in this feeble progress something began keeping pace with her, and again she had no idea what . . .

Now it was changing a little, coalescing, and yet . . . not becoming more clear, only more bewildering. The boy was in it now, he and his corruption were keeping company with Dominic's earlier presence in the unremembered dream, he was *there* . . . how could it be though, he was not born yet, or only just born . . . *I'll go mad,* she told Valeria thickly, then became aware of another change: her desperate refrain of *lie down, lie down,* had transposed itself to the stranger beat of *the end, the end.* "The end," she echoed it senselessly, then all at once knew something out of nowhere: *the end* did not mean the end of her marriage, it was something else, some other end buried deep in her very young years, maybe her childhood even . . .

Possessed by it, submerged, she reached her room totally forgetting her desire to rest. First putting away the damp shred of paper with automatic care, she fell weakly into a chair and sat unmoving and apparently unbreathing; with eyes wide open yet unseeing, locked once more in her trance of exhumation.

XI

To begin with then, say it was those two words *the end* that preoccupied without enlightening her in the least; say it was some experience of *the end* that had produced that moment of deathly terror in the attic; in that case she had better set to and dig it out before, unresolved, it converted itself into nightmares. The only trouble was that outside the decease of her mother and father which she had not actually seen—being at school when the first and asleep when the second died—she had had no *immediate* contact with the last of life, or at least that was how she interpreted the cryptic two words. Well then, if not actual death, had she witnessed any near-fatality or even severe calamity that had affected people she knew in greater or lesser degree? Shaking her head and still casting backward, she compounded for a lesser bargain. Had she ever been on the edge of a *stranger's* calamity? ever seen, at one or more removes, something that had frightened or distressed her deeply . . . ?

With the strain on her memory making her frown a little, all at once she was transported to a large unfamiliar room, empty-looking even with people in it, a . . . yes, a waiting-room. This had been when she was fifteen or so, not older; they had been living in London then, her mother was still alive. A doctor's waiting-room, no, an oculist's; lucky possessor of excellent sight, she had come to pick up a prescription for her father. In the dull high-ceilinged room she had sat bored and patient, inattentive to the magazine in her hands, her glance drifting now and then to the lofty double doors of the office . . .

All at once from behind these doors, and without the least premonitory sound, there burst a frightful clamour in a woman's voice, a wild clamour of protest going on and on; among the lesser stridencies of this voice she could hear the oculist speaking in a level tone, dry, inexorable . . . she remembered his name all at once: Dr Sweet, tall, thin, gentle-spoken. Some minutes later he opened one of the doors and beckoned her in for the prescription; in a shadowy corner of the office, which was very large, a stout old lady handsomely dressed sat leaning back in an armchair, a handkerchief to her eyes. And Val had not wanted to look or to see, it was only that the woman who was going to lose her sight (obviously) had been directly in her line of vision as she entered . . . was this the cause of what she had felt in the attic, this experience deliberately forgotten because it was so upsetting . . . ? Always staring blankly before her, she shook her head. Losing one's sight was of course a horror, an end of sorts, but not what her memory was rooting for so desperately. Or apparently not, the poor old lady refused to link herself with the blow she had received when seeing the naked boy: the blow of undefined terror, the toppling fear . . .

With an effort she freed her mind from the tragedy at Dr Sweet's, casting farther and farther back. Now a street was before her, in what city she had forgotten, but she remembered the woman who had fallen in front of a bus. With awful clarity she remembered her shabby look, a little dried-up thing lying on the ground with her shopping scattered about her; even more unbearably she remembered the cries she had uttered, just two incredibly hideous cries of astounding depth and volume considering the wizened body they came from; sounds full, orotund and enormous with fear of death . . .

The bus had stopped in time, stopped with not an inch to spare. The curious thing was that the street was loud with constant traffic, yet the cries stood out to her ear as unimpeded, as isolated, as if every other sound had been suspended meanwhile; of course this could not have been . . . and how old was she then? eleven, twelve? No matter, since this memory too served no purpose; had nothing at all to do with what she was dredging for, nothing at all . . .

Shaking her head like a fly-tormented horse and sinking lower in the lumpy armchair she went on confronting her peaceful, comfortable and orderly existence, demanding of it from where, from where on earth, she could have picked up anything so oppressively demanding as this, so tormenting . . . Something she had read? Her face lightened, then darkened immediately. It was either something she had seen happen, or something she had heard; of that much she was sure, for no reason. Yet in her life there had been nothing hidden, no furtive sexual experiments (even then she had been a vegetable, she reminded herself), nothing even moderately shameful. But at least she had got this far: she had seen it, or she had heard it. Only what, what, what . . .

A new thing possessed her all at once. Memory, wonderful and unpredictable, limited and limitless memory . . . It occurred to her now, for the first time, that people went to their graves unaware of a half, a quarter, of what their minds had stored up; ten thousand recollections, perhaps from infancy, unrealised till some particular experience, some special reminder, jarred them to the surface. Or—in her case—jarred it *toward* the surface. Only not enough, not sufficiently . . . Some impression perhaps from when she was three or four years old? So long ago, so deeply buried as to be beyond reach? Again, in strenuous rejection, she shook her head. It had not been an infantile or semi-infantile thing, she was willing to swear to it. Also, and all at once, she would swear to something else: that grown people had been talking nearby, talking with interest and animation. And how was it she had been present at this adult confabulation? This much was suddenly easy: when Mummy had people in to tea. It was during such restrained festivities that Val must be present to carry cups and help circulate plates of biscuits, it being Mummy's idea that this would help to overcome her gaucherie and shyness and instill social ease; Mummy had lots of ideas like that, immovable. No use, either, trying to get out of these loathsome occasions, her various rebellions had been firmly dealt with. Yet when the rite was more or less over and Mummy's attention was otherwise engaged . . .

With literal and unindulgent eyes she saw herself sliding off to a corner of the room and opening any book within reach, the house was bursting with books. What an unattractive brat she must have been, pale and undersized, prematurely addicted to reading. And opinionated, my God how opinionated; her diffidence with strangers did not extend to Papa and Mummy, to whom she discoursed on all and sundry with disgusting fluency and outspokenness. Papa had been amused but not Mummy, who would always pull her up short for unbecoming liberties of speech; this reproof had been especially severe on one occasion when she was holding forth on the subject of . . . of . . .

"Mrs Melwoosh," said someone aloud, belatedly waking her to her own voice. "Mrs Melwoosh . . ." Now from what remote cell of the mind had that name emerged? She had not thought of it in over twenty years . . . The name of course was Melhuish, but once this spelling had dawned on her eight-year-old horizon, the name was Melwoosh for good and all. A big woman, tall and broad and heavy, with a powerful

voice, a hearty laugh, streams and rivers of conversation . . .
She was in the living-room again, a book on her knees and
Mrs Melwoosh's accents getting between her and the book.
"Shut up," she chanted softly to herself, "shut up, shut up,"
also hating the woman for something else beside talking; talk-
ing and talking with her mouth full . . .

A gasp shook her, an indrawn breath like a gap. She was on
the track, the memory was leading somewhere . . . *fire!* Yes,
that was it, they had had a fire; not in the house but outside,
a gardener's shed had burned down late at night; responsibility was traced to a gardener's boy who had smoked there.
The bitterness of this remembrance was that she had seen
nothing of the fire, she had slept through all the glorious excitement, slept (again!) like a beastly dormouse. Was it the
recollection of her fury next day, when she yelled and
screamed at the top of her voice for having missed the fun:
was it this souvenir of unbearable loss (still faintly with her,
come to think) that accounted for her having buried the episode, forgotten it completely, till this very moment . . . ?
Once more she was trying to read against Mrs Melwoosh's
voice that went on and on, yet all at once—*now*, in this present moment—a different thing possessed her: a phrase com-
monplace in itself yet hammering at her again and again, and
the phrase was *heard but not listened to, heard but not listened to* . . . and out of her remoteness the thing wrapped
in years began stirring to life, the mummy was opening its
dusty eyes and looking at her . . .

The knock at the door, single and not loud, startled her
like cannon-shot; she sat unmoving for a moment, having to
travel back from over twenty years ago and needing time to
do it in, more time than she was being given . . .

The gentle knock was repeated, gently; she had thrown off
encumbering time not nearly completely as she went to answer.

XII

"Val," he said at once. "Could I talk to you another moment?"

"Of course." Seeing that he took a step backward, prepared to go downstairs again, all at once she realised her own exhaustion, as if she had been pursuing something at speed, running and running after it; in a dragging voice she murmured, "In here's all right." She stepped back, and he followed her in awkwardly.

"Won't you sit down—," she began, and at once he interrupted with, "No thanks, I've got to get back, I've . . ."

During the moment that his voice failed and he gathered himself to begin again, she saw an unfamiliar thing about him, then realised what it was. Anxiety: in his face, his voice, his carriage, anxiety wherever it could attach itself. And her immediate wonderment at this thing in him, totally unfamiliar, first of all dealt her hatred a destructive blow, then stirred her to another wonderment: that all her bitterness and desire for revenge were being submerged in . . . in . . .

"Val," he was saying, with a look of steeling himself to say it. "Are you going to have Palgrave take my job away from me?"

This thunderbolt dislocated her completely for an instant; as she stood silent, staring at him, he continued, "He would, you know."

His voice was dry; she knew this dryness for despair, just as she now recognised the nature of her own emotion.

"One word from you," he went on, "and he would."

"Dominic," she managed, undone with pity and wanting to burst out crying. *Poor man*, she thought bewilderingly and indistinctly, *poor defenceless man*, and steadied her voice with an effort. "As if I'd dream of doing anything like that, as if I'd *dream*—"

"Well, one doesn't know. I mean, I wouldn't blame you if you'd—"

It never occurred to me, she was about to interrupt, then for some reason suppressed it; outright lies at this moment were somehow beyond her. "I shan't interfere with your job, ever," she went on with new calmness. "So don't worry. And when we divorce—"

Strange that the death-dealing word was now powerless to affect her.

"—it'll be between us and no one else, Uncle Frederick won't have anything to do with it. I'll be the one that wants it," she concluded. "We'll think about grounds, both of us."

"Thank you, Val," he said after a moment. "Thank you."

His humility broke her heart all over again—or would have done, rather, if not for the other thing that possessed her more strongly than ever: the image of his being involved with Mrs Melwoosh and her mother's living-room all those years ago, he was in it somewhere, *somehow* . . .

"I'll be able to leave on schedule, pretty much," Dominic was saying. "In a couple of days he'll be fit to travel." He dismissed it, his voice changing again. "Forgive me, Val."

"Forgive you?" she echoed vaguely, from her mother's living-room.

"Well." His look was haggard, his laugh singularly unamused. "For everything of course, and also for my—my tackling you like this about the job. But I couldn't help it," he supplicated. "With—with someone else to take care of I had to know, I mean . . . you see, don't you?"

"Oh yes." Pain for his supplication rowelled her, and worse pain for her own degradation. She had planned to deprive him of his livelihood, do her best to see that he lost his job . . .

She awoke to see him take a step toward her. Involuntarily she became rigid; he stopped at once, balked in his intention— of gratitude? of an amicable handshake, a friendly kiss? Whatever it was her sudden look, quite unwilled, quite without anger, told him to keep his distance.

Again she was alone after the interruption, but this time not resenting nor damning it; far from breaking her train of thought, this time it had imbedded her—also Dominic—even more firmly among the women having tea with her mother. But how, how or why . . .

She happened to glance at her watch and received a mild shock. The first interview with Dominic, her visit upstairs and return here, her long journey back to the young lady, the girl, the child, the second interview with Dominic—had all that been accomplished in rather less than an hour? Time, a mystery as great as memory; time that could drag so painfully yet make all other species of transit look like lumbering drays, crawling Stone-Age wagons . . .

The unbelief and faint amusement vanished from her face. Again she was listening, with abstracted obedience rather than painfully, to what had diminished but never stopped during the second parley with Dominic. Mrs Melhuish going on and on, loud, positive and good-humoured; her voice so utterly complacent, so unshakably *sure* of itself . . .

The young man, having slipped down silently via the servants' staircase parallel to the course of the two bound for their first interview in the drawing-room, still remained at his listening-post as much as nearly an hour later. The effort he had made to get here was considerable, and the effort to return to his bed seemed so gigantic that he flinched away from it, continuing merely to sit on a step, motionless, while his mind swam and darted around what he had heard, or rather guessed at hearing. The main thing was that the cow could no longer be in the dark concerning himself and Dominic; not after the older man's anguished cry of *Maury!* and his anxious embrace . . .

A smirk of amusement touched his face and vanished. No time for pleasant reminiscence, what he had to do now was decide, decide on his course of action once he was on his feet again. The trouble, as always, was his imperfect understanding of their rotten language. Still, so far as he had picked up anything . . .

She had not offered Dominic a penny. That much he was sure of, which cast a decided shadow over his first rosy imaginings. The woman was in love with her husband, *follement amoureuse*, it was reasonable that she should fight to keep her claws on him, beg him to accept a big allowance, whatever he wanted if only, only he would not leave her . . .

She had failed to do anything of the sort, a strong disappointment; she had—so far as he could make out—given Dominic his congé, and in no uncertain terms. Yet the bright throb of hatred he felt for her had to be postponed, he could come back to it later. What could not be postponed was the consideration of his own advantage, the woman made less than no difference. What mattered now, what only mattered, was his future; whether to go back to Cecil or go to England with Dominic, and both of them *poor*, there was little choice between them . . . Yet if he accompanied the old one to England he might find a really rich admirer, it was a whole new field. In all this time he had not made up his mind which to do and he must decide, he must . . .

At this point his calculations were forcibly derailed by his treacherous body, the itching so furious that he longed to hook his nails into it and tear, tear . . . Except that the affected part, all up and down his left side, was too extensive, he was frightened to rip it open in any degree; his own instinct of self-preservation was as strong as the old one's prohibition against scratching. Better go upstairs and put butter on it, plenty of butter always stood on the bedside table. He would go up straightaway, yes, go up . . .

Instead he remained sitting there, pinned by an indecision which he realised, and a lassitude of which he was unaware. He must make up his mind quickly, quickly . . .

England: he had been there once on a day excursion, and the memory still horrified him. The gloom, the unseasonable cold and wet, the foolish unfamiliar faces making foolish unfamiliar sounds . . . One single advantage he had: the wife's refusal to go on with the marriage, so drop the dirty bitch from his calculations and go on from there. Dominic would have nothing, nothing in the world but his pay; it was ridiculous that a man so situated should expect a younger man to remain with him, to take on—no doubt—joint responsibility for the housework, the marketing, the cooking in some small *appartement* . . . "Ah, par example," he muttered aloud, "je ne serai qu'une bonne à tout faire." A feeble snort of laughter broke from him, and all at once his path was clear. Go with Dominic to his horrible country, remain with him long enough to achieve some new prospect, and then—

"Adieu, mon gars," he murmured aloud once more, "sois heureux!" preparing to lever himself up and then—all at once —pausing as his eye encountered the strangeness.

Out of the past came dates as the next image in her mind, stuffed dates from Fortnum and Mason, and the pale child loved them better than anything else in the world. Giant dates stuffed with marzipan and rolled in a special coarse brown sugar—and Mrs Melwoosh stuffing on them, exclaiming over their deliciousness from a full mouth, *rotten* manners by the way, and the unseen auditor keeping track of the havoc with murder in her heart. Mummy would not be going to Fortnum's for another few days and not one single date would be left, not one . . .

"Pig," she chanted aloud, but very softly. "Pig, pig, pig."

"But do you mean—"

Mummy's voice intruding on her ecstasy of baffled greed, then Mrs Melwoosh answering, piercing through the curtain of remembered anger and becoming—strangely—clearer, more and more distinct . . . And at that time she had paid no attention, none at all, but now she sat tight with listening, listening hard enough to crack her eardrums . . .

His ankles: even by this faint light, what was wrong with them? They were enormous, they had not looked like that only a short while ago . . . With a sort of mindless wonder he touched one of them; the impression of his finger remained there, as in dough. Rapidly he viewed himself, his knees, wrists and elbows, and beheld the same phenomenon; every joint in his body was puffed, blown up to twice its size, the body itself seemed enlarged. "Ah, merde," he said audibly, started rising again, and once more stopped dead; staring with complete stupefaction at something else, a worse thing that— this time—was not even visible.

"No hope," the loud assured voice was saying with certainty and relish. "No hope at all."

"But young, you said, a *young* man—?"

"Very young, strong as an ox and perfectly magnificent, young and big and strong—"

Still talking about fires, were they? Her obscuring rage had made her lose the thread completely, she was impaled on her vision of loss . . .

"Oh! just one of these gorgeous dates left." Mrs Melwoosh's voice had turned infantile and cajoling. "Do you think I dare—"

"Oh *please* do!"

Mummy couldn't help herself, she had had to say it. "Rotten Mrs Melwoosh," the little girl hissed between her teeth on which she wore a brace; she could feel the vanished brace now, she was the little girl in the corner and the woman sitting in the chair, at one and the same time. "Rotten pig."

"But you said," Mummy was continuing, "it was slight—"

Invisible, yes, the thing inside of him; his arms and legs were locked, his body was leaden; when he made another effort to get to his feet, something ran like lightning all through him. Not pain, no, more frightening than pain: an enormous failing and falling, a draining away, a giant dizziness . . . and with it the itching renewed itself and became nightmare, a screaming torment. He must get up, get upstairs quickly and put butter on it, butter, heaps of butterbutterbutter. . . . .

". . . slight?" That was Mummy again. "The harm done was very slight?"

"Entirely, it was entirely—"

What was the next word? It must have been unfamiliar to her, it delayed to come forward. Trifling? no. Minor? no. Superficial? That was it, that must have been it . . .

And as if it were the key, all the rest of it was there, clear and entire; heard but not listened to, sunk deep in her memory without her knowledge and lying there, whole and entire, till this moment of its baleful resurrection.

"But you said he was unhurt?" Mummy insisted. "Otherwise?"

"Completely unhurt, just that very slight scorching all up and down his left side, I *think* his left side—"

"But why?" Mummy demanded, fretful. "A boy or hardly more than a boy, in excellent health—?"

"Perfect health, my dear, perfect." *Rude* Mrs Melwoosh, interrupting, she was always doing it. "And all the same no hope for him, not a vestige of hope—Oh my word, just see the time! I must fly." With remains of the date still cumbering her speech she was putting on her jacket, to judge by the small rustling. "Bye-bye, my love, a thousand thanks for the heavenly tea."

Heavenly dates you mean, you nasty old stinker, thought the unseen contributor, and became daring through mere excess of venom. *Hog.*

"But I still don't understand." Mummy was fighting, wearisomely, a rearguard action. "Why he should—"

"Die?" blared Mrs Melwoosh. "My handbag, where is— Oh, here." She had picked it up, apparently. "You can't live, can you my dear, with half the pores of your body out of commission?"

S